# The Night They Stole the Stanley Cup

Roy MacGregor

An M&S Paperback Original from
McClelland & Stewart Ltd.
*The Canadian Publishers*

**For Doug and Mark Sprott,**
**who brought me back into minor hockey**

The author is grateful to Doug Gibson, who thought up this series, and to Alex Schultz, who pulls it off.

An M&S Paperback Original from McClelland & Stewart Ltd.

**Library and Archives Canada Cataloguing in Publication**

MacGregor, Roy, 1948–
    The night they stole the Stanley Cup

(The Screech Owls series)
ISBN-10: 0-7710-5626-5    ISBN-13: 978-0-7710-5626-0

I. Title.  II. Series: MacGregor, Roy, 1948–    .
The Screech Owls series.

PS8575.G74N55 1995    jC813'.54    C95-932303-1
PZ7.M33Ni 1995

We acknowledge the financial support of the Government of Canada through the Book Publishing Industry Development Program and that of the Government of Ontario through the Ontario Media Development Corporation's Ontario Book Initiative. We further acknowledge the support of the Canada Council for the Arts and the Ontario Arts Council for our publishing program.

Cover illustration by Gregory C. Banning
Typesetting by M&S, Toronto

Printed and bound in Canada

McClelland & Stewart Ltd.
*The Canadian Publishers*
75 Sherbourne Street
Toronto, Ontario
M5A 2P9
www.mcclelland.com

    13 14 15 16    09 08 07

MATS SUNDIN CHEWED HIS NAILS – JUST LIKE TRAVIS Lindsay. Mats Sundin's hands were twice as big as Travis's, but the nails were the same, bitten to the quick. It surprised Travis; he had never imagined that a National Hockey League superstar would ever have anything to worry about. Nails, like life, would be perfect. But here was the best player on the Toronto Maple Leafs, one of the best players in the NHL, and he was no different from more than half the players on the Screech Owls – nervous and fidgeting when it came to waiting around in the dressing room. Travis liked him immediately.

"Good to meet you, Travis."

Travis swallowed hard. He had imagined perhaps getting Mats Sundin's autograph on the card he had in his vest pocket, but that was supposed to involve a lot of work getting Sundin's attention. Yet here was the great Mats Sundin greeting *him* as if it were the most natural thing in the world.

"Hi," Travis said. He wondered if Mats Sundin had even heard him.

The Screech Owls had come to Toronto to play in "The Little Stanley Cup," a huge tournament that was being held over the March school break. Novice and peewee and bantam teams had been invited from Ontario and Quebec, as well as from New York and Michigan. Each team was guaranteed three games, four if they made it into the playoffs, and most were also planning to attend a Leafs game.

The Screech Owls, like the Leafs, had gone through a rebuilding season. Sarah Cuthbertson, the team captain, had moved on permanently to the Toronto Aeros after the Lake Placid tournament. There had even been a story about Sarah in the *Toronto Star* saying she was a shoo-in for the Canadian women's hockey team at the 1998 Winter Olympics.

Matt Brown and his loudmouth father were also missing. Mr. Brown had wanted Matt on another team, where he thought his son might be appreciated a bit more. Mr. Brown had, as usual, missed the point. Matt was greatly appreciated, especially his wicked shot, but Mr. Brown was not. Hockey games this season had been more enjoyable for everyone – fans as well as players. No Mr. Brown screaming at the referees. No Mr. Brown pounding the glass and shouting at them to get out there and "kick butt!"

Muck was back as coach, of course. Back and still the same. It was the Screech Owls who had changed, but not nearly as much as some of the teams they played against. Nish and Data and Willie were all still Owls, along with most of the others, but as well as Sarah and Matt, Zak and Mario were gone, as were goaltenders Guy Boucher – still hanging on as the back-up goalie for the double-A team – and Sareen Goupa, who was now the starting goalie for the town's new women's team.

With Guy and Sareen missing, the Screech Owls had taken on Jennie Staples and a new kid in town, Jeremy Weathers, who had a terrific glove hand. Derek Dillinger had moved up onto the first line to take over Sarah's spot between Travis and Dmitri Yakushev – who was *faster* this year, if anything – and the new second-line centre was Gordie Griffith, whose skating bursts were finally catching up to his growth spurts. The new third-line centre was Andy Higgins, a big, mean guy whose voice was already dropping. Travis didn't much care for Andy. He wasn't quite sure why – he just didn't like him.

The new second-line left-winger was Liz Moscovitz, a good friend of Sarah's, and the new third-line winger was Chantal Larochelle, whose family had just moved to town from Montreal. The new defenceman was Lars Johanssen, who'd been born in Sweden and had come to Canada when his father was sent over to run the chip-board factory just outside town. It was Lars's father who had arranged for the team to attend the Leafs' practice. Back in Sweden, Mr. Johanssen had worked – and once played – with Mats Sundin's father.

Mats Sundin treated Lars like a long-lost cousin and gave him a stick that had been signed by every one of the Leafs. Then he had taken the team into the actual dressing room, where some of the players were still sitting around and others were fixing up their sticks for the next game.

Travis thought he had died and gone to heaven. He could not stop staring at the players as they worked on their sticks.

One of the players had the tip of a new stick underneath the door frame and was pulling up on the handle to make a quick little curve at the very end of the blade. Travis bent down and stared, fascinated.

"You do this, too?" the man asked.

Travis looked up, startled. *It was Doug Gilmour.*

The Leafs' captain was smiling back at Travis. Travis could only shake his head, no. He couldn't talk. What could he say to Doug Gilmour? *I have your poster up in my room? I know a guy who's got your rookie card from St. Louis?*

But it didn't seem as if he had to say anything. Doug Gilmour was still smiling. Now he was pulling out the stick and trying it, leaning down hard and bending it so he could check the whip in the shaft. Then he flicked a used roll of tape and it flew hard against the wall and bounced off, straight into a garbage can.

"How come I can't do that in games?" Gilmour asked.

Travis looked around. There was no one else there. That meant Doug Gilmour had to be talking to *him*! Still, he couldn't answer.

"You a left shot?" Gilmour asked.

Travis finally spoke: "Y—yeah."

"Here, then – you give it a try."

Travis took the stick. It felt like King Arthur's sword in his hand: magical, powerful, but too big and heavy for him. Doug Gilmour threw down a fresh roll of tape. "Let's see your shot."

Travis almost fainted. Doug Gilmour was asking to see *his* shot! He stickhandled the tape back and forth a couple of times and then fired it. It hit with a dull thud against the wall, fell to the floor, and rolled away.

"Good wrister," Gilmour said.

"I've got a better slapshot," Travis said. He wasn't certain he did, but he felt he'd better explain that he wasn't quite as weak as his shot had sounded.

"Then you'd better have this stick," Doug Gilmour said. "It works better for you than me."

Travis couldn't believe it. Doug Gilmour was grinning, but not laughing at him. He was serious.

"You're giving this to me?" Travis asked.

"Only if you want it," Doug Gilmour said. "Here – let me sign it for you."

Gilmour took a Sharpie pen off the bench by the skate sharpener and signed his name and number: Doug Gilmour – 93. He handed the stick back to Travis.

"There you go. It's yours now."

The stick was alive in Travis's hands, as if it held an electric current. He could hardly believe this was happening. It all felt like a dream. He felt he was floating. He felt dizzy

"Thanks," Travis said. It didn't seem enough.

"Any time, buddy," Doug Gilmour said, and smiled. "Thanks" seemed like enough to him.

The Leafs' captain went back into the training room, where no one but the players and trainers and equipment workers were allowed, and Travis – hanging onto his stick for dear life – raced off to find the rest of the team.

They weren't in the dressing room. They weren't in the corridor. But there were bright lights shining from out in the arena, and when he got there he could see television cameramen around the bench area, where a lot of Screech Owls jacket backs could be seen.

Travis hurried over. The team was gathered in a semicircle around Mats Sundin, who was answering questions. The television camera crews were recording, and several reporters were also there, writing very quickly in small notebooks.

"Do you have another job you go to?" Fahd Noorizadeh asked.

Travis could see Nish turn to Willie Granger and roll his eyes. A typical Fahd question. What would he ask next: Do you do up your own skates?

Mats Sundin laughed good-naturedly: "This is my only job – it's more than enough to keep me busy."

"Who's your favourite player?" Gordie Griffith asked.

"Doug Gilmour, of course," Mats Sundin answered, again laughing.

Nish moved in, grinning: "What do you think of Don Cherry?"

Travis couldn't believe Nish could be so stupid. Everyone knew what Don Cherry had said on "Coach's Corner" about the Wendel Clark trade that brought Sundin to Toronto from Quebec. Everyone knew what the "Hockey Night in Canada" analyst had been saying for as long as they could remember about European players faking injuries and taking dives and never coming through in the Stanley Cup playoffs.

"I think Don Cherry is a very funny comedian," Sundin said.

"A 'comedian'?" Nish asked.

"Yes – he's very funny. But you can't take him seriously."

Fahd had another Fahd question: "Can you speak Swedish?"

Mats Sundin blinked, not believing his ears. "Here's another comedian," he laughed. "Just like Don Cherry."

Fahd didn't get it. "Can you?" he repeated.

Mats Sundin shrugged and turned to Lars Johanssen. Mats began talking very fast, in Swedish, to Lars, who giggled and said something very quickly back to Mats.

One of the reporters called out: "What're you two saying?"

Mats Sundin laughed. "I asked my good friend Lars if his team have given him a nickname yet."

"And have they?" another reporter asked.

They hadn't – until Nish jumped in.

"We call him Cherry," Nish shouted.

Everyone – including Lars – laughed. The reporters scribbled it down. The cameras turned their floodlights on Nish, who never even flinched.

"Wayne Nishikawa," he called out to the reporters.

"N–I–S–H–I . . ."

## 2

"WHO TOOK MY UNDERWEAR?"

Travis had never heard such a ridiculous question. Nish was still in his pyjamas while everyone else was dressed and ready to head off for the first game of the Little Stanley Cup. They had ten minutes to be in the hotel lobby – and Nish hadn't even brushed his teeth yet.

"Somebody took my underwear. Come on, now! This is ridiculous!"

I'll say it is, thought Travis. Ridiculous that Nish could be thirteen years old and still not know how to pack for a road trip. He had already emptied the entire contents of his suitcase out on the bed he and Travis were sharing and ploughed through his clothes like a dog rooting through garbage. Enough T-shirts to supply the team – each one proof that he had played in hockey tournaments everywhere from Lake Placid to Quebec City – pants and sweatshirts and socks and comic books and deodorant and toothpaste and toothbrush – but no underwear. He'd only brought the pair he was wearing, and now he couldn't even find them!

"This is a SICK joke!" Nish said. He was getting upset.

"*You're* a sick joke," said Willie Granger. Willie was sharing the other bed with Data, Nish's defence partner. "You can't even pack a suitcase."

"You should have had your mom do it," said Data, who was growing a bit anxious about the deadline for being in the lobby.

Nish held up his hands. "Stop! Just sit on it, okay? We know they were here last night."

"*You* know they were here last night," corrected Willie.

"Who else was here?"

"Who *wasn't* here?" said Travis. He was right. Their room had been like a bus terminal. Everyone had run down after they checked in to see the four who'd lucked into a suite when the hotel ran out of regular rooms. There was a bedroom off a sitting room, two televisions, and a small kitchen with a refrigerator. Everyone had jealously checked out everything in the suite, but surely not Nish's underwear.

"Okay!" Nish shouted. He was beginning to panic. "We know they're here somewhere."

"I'm not touching your shorts!" Data shouted back.

"No one's asking you to *touch* them – just point when you find them!" Nish said. He was getting testy. "Travis and Data, you two do the other room and kitchen. Willie will help me do the bathroom and bedroom. Look absolutely everywhere – and *hurry*!"

They didn't like doing it, but what choice did they have? Nish had to have underwear, and he was far too big and heavy to wear anyone else's. So they began looking, Nish and Willie taking the bedroom apart bit by bit, and Travis and Data going over the sitting room and the kitchen.

"You look in the kitchen cupboards," Data said. "I'll check in here behind all the cushions."

"We didn't use the cupboards," Travis said.

"Maybe someone threw them there as a joke."

Unconvinced, Travis began looking. He checked each cupboard – nothing. He checked all the drawers – no underwear.

The only thing left to check was the refrigerator. Surely, no. He opened the door – no luck. He flicked open the freezer compartment: *there was something inside*. Whatever it was, it was crumpled up and covered with frost. He poked at it. It was as hard as a rock. Then he recognized the blue diamond pattern of Nish's boxer shorts.

"They're here!" Travis called out.

Nish came running into the room, already dropping his pyjamas. "Gimme them!"

"You'll have to chip them out," said Travis.

Nish stopped dead in his tracks, his eyes big as hockey pucks.

"What kind of a sick joke is this!" he shouted.

He pulled at the shorts and they cracked –

frozen. He pulled again and they gave. He began unfolding them, the frost drifting in the air as they bent in his hands.

"Who would do this?"

"Not me."

"Wasn't me."

"I never."

It wasn't any of them, either. They all knew that. Who'd have the guts to touch Nish's shorts in the first place?

"This isn't fair," Nish wailed. "I got nothing else to wear!"

"Then you've got no choice, do you?" Data said. "We gotta roll – and quick."

The others went down to the lobby ahead of Nish. Muck was already there, checking his watch. The rest of the team and some of the parents were standing around and waiting as well.

"Where's Nishikawa?" Muck asked.

"He's coming," said Travis.

Everyone waited. Finally the elevator doors opened, and out walked Nish, his face in agony, his steps uncertain.

"What's with him?" Muck asked. "Got cold feet over the tournament?"

"Not exactly," Travis answered.

## 3

TRAVIS WAS BEGINNING TO UNDERSTAND WHY HE had such a bad feeling about the new centre, Andy Higgins. He seemed to swear a lot – much more than necessary – and he sometimes smelled of cigarette smoke. But neither of those points troubled Travis. Most of the kids swore a bit. And some of them – even Nish, his best friend – thought smoking was okay, even if they didn't do it. No, what really bothered Travis was that he believed Andy Higgins was stealing.

He'd noticed things before. Data brought his older brother's tape deck to the dressing room and said it was the Screech Owls' to keep; his brother had moved on to a CD player. They were each supposed to bring in a tape for playing before and after games. Just like the pros. Travis had saved his allowance and bought the Tragically Hip, and some of the others had brought in a variety of other tapes: Counting Crows, some rap, the Barenaked Ladies, and even, to a loud chorus of boos directed Fahd's way, Michael Jackson.

One tape apiece. Except for Andy Higgins.

He'd brought in close to a dozen. All brand new, all still in their wrappers. Most were recent hits and, naturally, they got the most play, which had the effect of putting Andy in charge of the team tape recorder and making him instantly popular. But not with Travis. He'd figured out that Andy had to have spent roughly $150 to buy those particular tapes, and that hardly seemed like allowance money.

Now, in Toronto, Andy was walking around the dressing room flicking a lighter at everyone. It was brand new, with the CN Tower on it. Just like the ones Travis and Nish had seen in the hotel gift shop. But they would never have sold a lighter to a thirteen-year-old kid. He could have swiped it, however, and that's exactly what Travis thought he had done.

Travis left the dressing room and went out to clear his head. The Little Stanley Cup was being played in more than a dozen Toronto arenas, and the Screech Owls had come to play their first game in St. Michael's Arena, where so many NHLers had played their early hockey. He walked alongside the glass display case near the snack bar, looking at the old photographs under the sign "THE TRADITION LIVES ON": Red Kelly, Joe Primeau, Tim Horton, Frank Mahovlich, Dave Keon.

And then, Terrible Ted himself. Ted Lindsay, with the crooked smile and the hair that looked as if it had been parted with a protractor. Terrible Ted Lindsay smiling back at Travis Lindsay, his distant relative. Travis wondered if perhaps *he* would one day play here for St. Mike's? He imagined himself moving on to play in the NHL and being inducted into the St. Mike's Hall of Fame, right alongside Terrible Ted. Travis couldn't think of anything he wouldn't trade to get there – well, maybe except for Doug Gilmour's stick.

When Travis returned to the dressing room, everyone had started to dress. Nish was sitting wrapped in his towel. He had his shorts hanging off the blade of his stick directly in front of a hot-air vent.

"They can't still be cold!" Travis said.

"*Damp*," said Nish. "I catch the guy who did this, he's good as dead."

"The guy who did that is probably already dead from touching them!" Wilson shouted. Everyone laughed. Everyone but Nish, who just said, "Very funny."

Travis couldn't tell whether he was really annoyed or enjoying the attention. It was always difficult to say with Nish.

The Owls' assistant coach, Barry, stuck his head in the door and told them to hurry up. The room went silent as the team got down to the serious work of dressing. What Barry meant, but would never say, was that the boys should hurry so the girls – Jennie, Liz, and Chantal – could join them in time to put on their skates and get ready for Muck's pep talk.

Travis always liked these moments best. He loved dressing. He felt, at times, like a machine being assembled: underwear, protector, garter, left shin pad, right shin pad, socks, attach socks to garter, pants on loose, skates on loose, watch until Nish closes his eyes and begins rocking back and forth – Nish's way of getting ready – then tighten skates, tie pants, tighten belt on pants, shoulder pads, elbow pads, neck guard, lay sweater in lap, think, pull sweater over head and make hideous face at Nish when hidden by sweater, wait, then helmet, click on face mask, gloves, stick, and *ready*. Always the same order, always the same timing. A machine waiting only for someone to flick the switch.

Flicking the switch was Muck's job. He always said something – never too complicated, never overly critical, like a teacher's last words before an exam. In Round One of the Little Stanley Cup, the Screech Owls would be playing the Junior River Rats from Albany, New York, a peewee version of the minor pro team with the best sweater and cap logo Travis had ever seen: a snarling rat holding a hockey stick.

The three girls came in, Jennie walking stiff-legged in her goalie pads like a robot, Liz and Chantal bouncing lightly on their skates. Travis smiled quietly to himself. He had noticed the "bounce" lately, and not just from the girls, but from Nish and Dmitri too, and, he had to admit, even from himself at times. The bounce was a signal: you were a *hockey* player.

Muck came in. Muck always dressed as if he were going down to Canadian Tire to pick up some wood screws. No fancy hockey jacket with badges all over it. No tie. No clipboard filled with notes. Nothing. Just Muck. Just the way he'd always been.

"Okay," Muck said. Instantly the room went silent. Muck never had to raise his voice, that's how much respect the players had for their coach.

"This is a team we haven't seen before. I don't expect they're going to give us too much trouble, but by the same token I don't expect us to do anything but play our game. That means what, Nish?"

Nish had been staring down between his knees, concentrating.

"'Stay in position,'" Nish quoted. It was one of Muck's favourite phrases, and Nish almost sounded like the coach when he said it. Travis knew why Muck had asked Nish; everyone knew who the worst offender was if a game was too easy. Nish would suddenly think he was Paul Coffey, rushing end to end with the puck.

"That's right," agreed Muck. "*Stay in position.* No dumb moves. No 'glory hogs.'"

Nish looked up abruptly, surprised that Muck

would use the same expression his teammates used when they were ragging on him. Muck stared right back, a small grin at the corners of his mouth.

"I want to see passing. I want to see you use your points. I want to see everyone – and I mean *everyone* – coming back to help out your defence and goaltender.

"Now let's go."

**4**

TRAVIS DID HIS LITTLE BOUNCE–SKIP AS HE TURNED the first corner on the new ice. Just ahead of him, Nish did the same. At the next corner, he saw Liz do one too, her second thrust of her right skate digging deep, the blade sizzling as it cut into the fresh ice and left its mark. She was a beautiful skater.

Travis wished the ice could always be fresh. He loved the feel of it, but he also loved the stories in it, the way he could read how someone had shifted from forward to backward skating, the way a long, hard-driving stride threw snow.

The River Rats may have had beautiful uniforms, but they could not skate at all like the Screech Owls. Travis knew from the warm-up that it would be an easy game for the Owls – but perhaps not for him. He'd failed to hit the cross-bar while taking shots at the empty net. He knew it was silly, but he liked to start each game with his good-luck sign.

The River Rats had one pure skater – one player with the little bounce-skip as he came out onto the ice – and a few big players, but little else.

Travis's line started. Derek won the face-off and put the puck back to Nish, who drew the forechecker to him and then hit Data with a perfect pass. Data put the puck off the boards so it floated in behind the River Rats' defence, and Dmitri, with an astonishing burst of speed, jetted around the turning defender, picked up the puck, and put a high slapshot in under the glove arm of the Albany goaltender.

Muck then took Travis's line off. An eleven-second shift. Muck hated to embarrass anyone, either on his own team or on any other. (Well, perhaps with the exception of Nish, who needed regular embarrassing.) The shift had been so short that from the bench Travis could actually see the play in the new ice: Dmitri's quick jump past the defence, the marks where the defence had turned too late, Dmitri's perfect trail followed by the defenceman's stumbling chase, the very point from where Dmitri had shot – all still laid out on the ice like a connect-the-dots puzzle.

At the end of the first, the Screech Owls were up 4–0 on a second breakaway by Dmitri, a good shot from the slot by Gordie Griffith, and a hard shot from the point by Lars Johanssen. At this last goal, the entire bench had erupted in shouts for "Cherry!" when everyone realized Lars had scored his first goal as a Screech Owl. It was a good thing the others were scoring, Travis thought. Even with such weak opposition, he couldn't break out of his scoring slump.

Jennie had all of two shots to handle, and one of them a long dump from centre ice. Apart from their one good skater, the River Rats were simply out of their league, outclassed and already out of the game. Muck couldn't have been more displeased.

Travis thought he knew why. Muck hated a game like this at any time – too easy, too tempting to players like Nish to start playing shinny – but he would hate it even more as the first game of an important tournament. He would say it made the Screech Owls too confident, too easy to beat in the second game, which is the game that usually decides whether a team continues on the championship side or the consolation side of the tournament. From the moment the puck had dropped in this match, Muck was probably more worried about Game Two than Game One.

Muck began giving extra ice time to the third line. But Andy, Jesse, and Chantal were still too dominant for the Albany team. Andy scored a fabulous, end-to-end goal, finishing with an unnecessary fall-to-your-knees, fist-pumping celebration that made Muck decide to yank them off as well.

Muck finally told the Screech Owls to ease up. With a minute to go, and the Screech Owls up

7−0, the River Rats' one good player took a pass at centre. Data had been pinching up ice and was caught behind the play, leaving only Nish back between Jennie and the skater.

Nish was skating backwards as fast as possible. The ice was old now and choppy, and he dug in as best he could. But he could not cut off the swift River Rat without turning toward him and shifting from backward to forward skating.

Just as Nish made his move, the skater made his. He pushed toward Nish instead of going away from him, and as he did so he flipped the puck so it rolled high over Nish's stick and fell flat behind him. The skater simply hopped over Nish as he fell in desperation, picked up the puck, walked in, and pulled Jennie to her right before dropping an easy backhander in behind her.

The game ended 7−1. The players shook hands – Jennie congratulating the scorer on his play – and then headed for the dressing room.

Muck came in a few moments later, not at all pleased.

"What do you have to say for yourself, Nish?" Muck asked.

"What'dya mean?" Nish asked.

Muck smiled. "You got deked out of your underwear out there."

Nish shook his head in disgust. "He can have them."

## 5

"YOU GOTTA COME AND SEE THIS!"

Travis had rarely seen Nish so excited. And certainly never so early in the morning. Travis had just finished showering and was getting dressed to go down for breakfast. It had been a quiet night; the team was tired from the excitement of the first game, if not the actual playing of the game, and everyone had gone to bed early.

Nish, of course, had tried to turn on the late-night sex movies, but all the television screen would say was: "ADULT MOVIES HAVE BEEN BLOCKED BY REQUEST. PLEASE CALL THE FRONT DESK FOR ACCESS." He had tried his old trick of pulling off the cable wires and re-wiring the remote box, but again it hadn't worked. Finally he had called the front desk and in a low voice pretended he was Muck giving the hotel permission for the kids to watch sex movies. That hadn't worked either.

Now here he was, flushed and on fire about something.

"You gotta come see, Trav!"

Travis pulled on his Red Wings track pants and a T-shirt and chased, barefoot, after Nish, who was already running down the hall backwards, signalling Travis to follow.

On the floor below, Nish came to a door and knocked. Not a normal knock, but three long knocks followed by two quick ones. A special code? What was this? Travis wondered.

Nish held his finger to his mouth, signalling quiet. As he hadn't been saying anything, Travis could only shake his head.

They could hear someone on the other side. Travis had the sense he was being checked out through the little spy glass in the door. Then it opened slowly. It was Data. He and Nish must have come down earlier, while Travis was in the shower. But why so secretive?

Data opened the door the rest of the way. Nish and Travis entered and Data closed the door quietly, still acting mysteriously. It was a smaller room, not a suite like Travis and the others had lucked into. Wilson and Fahd were standing at the far side of the room, staring down at something on the bed by the window. The door to the bathroom opened and out came Andy Higgins.

Andy seemed to be trying to look tough even though there was nobody there to impress. He barely looked at Travis.

Travis went over to the bed and looked. Arranged as if on display were several chocolate bars, three more CN Tower lighters, a Blue Jays mug, a brand-new Toronto Maple Leafs cap – the price tag still on it – a deck of cards still in its wrapper, and a pack of Belmont Milds cigarettes.

"Tell the world, why don't you," Andy said to Nish. He seemed both angry and proud at the same time.

Travis asked the obvious: "Where'd all this come from?"

"The lobby gift shop," Nish answered.

Nish didn't have to add that they were stolen goods. Travis knew without asking. He felt suddenly hot, prickly, like the room had only heat and no air and he had to get out. But he knew, too, that he couldn't let his panic show. He was captain. He was responsible.

"The old lady on cash is blind as a bat," offered Andy. He obviously wanted it understood that he had done the stealing.

"How'd you get the smokes?" Nish wanted to know. Nish also looked flushed. But from excitement.

"She was sorting the newspapers – I just reached over and grabbed a pack."

Nish was obviously impressed: "Shoulda grabbed one for me."

Travis looked sharply at him. *Don't encourage*

*him*, he wanted to say. But Nish was already lost. The last time Travis had seen that look in Nish's face was when the team had been in the Maple Leafs' dressing room. Nish was star-struck – with a shoplifter!

Travis felt like a clothes dryer: standing still but spinning inside. He knew he couldn't show his nervousness or they would laugh at him. He knew they would never listen to him if he told Andy to put the stuff back. But he was captain – he had some responsibility to the Screech Owls. And he knew if some of the team got in trouble, Muck would want to know where his team captain had been and whether he had known what was going on. No matter the outcome, Travis already felt he was going to be in the wrong.

Finally, he steeled himself: "You shouldn't have done that to her, Andy."

Andy just laughed. Nish laughed with him, not even knowing why.

"It's not *hers*," Andy sneered. "You think a big hotel chain like this is going to miss a few lighters? What kind of a wimp are you anyway, Lindsay?"

Travis could see he wasn't going to get any support. Nish was all but sneering himself. Data was playing with one of the lighters.

"Take one," Andy said to Data.

Data seemed surprised, pleased. "You mean it?"

"Sure," Andy said. "Plenty more where that one came from."

The boys all laughed at the joke.

Everyone, that is, but Travis Lindsay, team captain . . . wimp.

## 6

MR. DILLINGER, THE TEAM MANAGER, HAD DONE A wonderful job of organizing the team's time in Toronto. They'd been to the Leafs' practice, and they were going to see the game against the Blackhawks. It wasn't the Red Wings, but it was still an Original Six team, and Chicago had two of Travis's favourite players: Jeremy Roenick and Ed Belfour.

Mr. Dillinger had also laid out a full program of sightseeing for both the players and those parents who had come on the trip. Parents and players weren't always interested in the same things. This morning the players were going to walk down Yonge Street on their way to the CN Tower, and they were all going up to the top – even Nish, who hated heights.

Travis should have been more excited, but all he could think about was what to do about Andy Higgins. No one else seemed bothered by it, or maybe they just wouldn't say. Who wanted to be called a wimp by their teammates?

It was a beautiful early spring day for the walk.

Since they could see the CN Tower from the hotel and there was no chance of anyone getting lost, Muck and Mr. Dillinger said the players could walk on their own, so long as they stayed in groups. Andy joined Travis's bunch, which both surprised Travis and bothered him.

They had barely gone a block when Andy stopped, took a cigarette out of his shirt pocket, and made a big show of lighting it.

"Muck better not see you," Travis said. He thought he sounded like his mother.

Andy blew smoke out and waved it away as if he'd like to wave Travis away too.

"'*Muck better not see you,*'" Andy whined, impersonating Travis. The others laughed. "Muck's the *coach*, not my *mother.*"

Travis half-felt like walking away, but he couldn't. He knew he had to stay with the group. He had to.

"You guys?" Andy said, holding the stolen cigarettes out and raising his eyebrows as he offered them around. Nish helped himself – "For later," he added sheepishly – but no one else reached for one. Travis wouldn't even acknowledge the offer.

"Suit yourselves," Andy said. "Which way're we going?"

"I'm checking out the Zanzibar," Nish announced.

"What's the Zanzibar?" Data asked. Travis had no idea either.

"Just the biggest strip joint in the world, that's all," Nish said, as if it were common knowledge.

"Yeah, I heard about it," said Andy.

Travis knew he was lying.

"My cousin told me about it," Nish said. "A hundred bare-naked women."

Travis closed his eyes. Nish was, as usual, out of control. Mr. Markle had told their class this year that puberty would be coming on soon for some of them. He talked about shaving and voices dropping and moods – but he had never said anything about Nish being committed to a psychiatric hospital.

"And how do you expect to get in?" Travis asked.

"I'll worry about that when I get there," Nish said.

They walked on down Toronto's busiest street, the sights and sounds and smells almost too much for a head to hold at once. The hint of good weather had brought out the sidewalk vendors: hot dogs, jewellery, T-shirts, sunglasses. There were kids not much older than himself with green hair and safety pins through their cheeks. There was a man reading aloud from the Bible and another screaming in a strange language at everyone who passed by.

"Isn't this fantastic?" Nish shouted.

Travis didn't know if that was quite the right word for it, but it was *something* – fascinating and frightening at the same time.

"*There it is!*" Nish shouted again, pointing ahead of them. They could see the sign, "ZANZI-BAR," and they could see a rough-looking crowd milling around the photographs of the dancers on the front of the building. Loud rock music burst out every time the door opened and closed. Travis felt alarmed – but also curious. He hadn't the nerve to walk up and look in.

But Nish did. He elbowed his way through the crowd and stood, hands in pockets, staring at the photographs as if he were shopping for something and knew exactly what he wanted. Andy joined him, his cigarette now burned down near the filter. He stomped it out on the sidewalk and spat. The two of them looked ridiculous, Travis thought.

Travis, Gordie, Fahd, and Data hurried on past the bar and stood waiting nervously.

Finally Andy came along, putting a fresh cigarette in his mouth. He stopped to light it, acting as if nothing at all was happening, when he knew perfectly well that the others were almost in full panic about Nish's whereabouts.

"Where is he?" Gordie shouted. Andy raised

his eyebrows as if he hadn't heard. But of course he had.

"What'd you do with him?" Data asked, smiling.

"He's probably on stage by now," Andy chuckled.

"*He is?*" Gordie and Data said at the same time. Andy nodded, drawing deep on his cigarette, then choking. *Good*, Travis thought.

Before they had time to ask anything else, the crowd behind them parted as if a mad dog were coming through, and out from the middle burst Nish in full flight, a huge, angry man close behind him shaking his fist. He swung at Nish but missed, Nish's thick legs churning on down the street and past the other boys.

At top speed, Nish turned the first corner he came to, but his hip caught the edge of a vendor's table, flipping it as he tore by. The table, covered with sunglasses, spilled out onto the street, blocking the man from the Zanzibar, who came to a halt and between gasps for air screamed after Nish.

"And don't you ever . . . try that again, punk!"

The vendor was tempted to take up the chase but turned instead to his more-immediate problem: a street covered with sunglasses. After looking twice in the direction Nish had run, he cursed and bent down to pick up his spilled goods. People in the street, including the boys, came to help, and soon the table was back up and the vendor was trying to pop a lens back into a pair of glasses.

"Thanks," the man said. He didn't look too pleased.

The boys hurried on down the street, the CN Tower periodically looming high to their right when the skyscrapers gave way to open space. They knew they would eventually come across Nish again. At least they hoped they would. If someone didn't kill him first.

"*Hey!*"

They looked across the street. It was Nish, waving. They crossed at the light and joined him. He was red as the stoplight and puffing hard. He must have crossed and doubled back. He kept looking back up the street for his assailant, but he was grinning.

"What happened?" said Data.

"Did you get in?" Gordie asked.

"'Course I got in," Nish said angrily. Travis knew Nish too well not to know the truth. He hadn't even come close.

"What'dya see?" Data asked.

"More'n you can imagine, sunshine."

Travis knew it was really just as much as *Nish* could imagine. Some people could look at a cloud and see things; Nish could look at an empty blue sky and see anything he wanted.

"You'll probably need these after that eyeful," Andy said.

He was handing Nish a brand-new pair of sunglasses. He'd swiped them when they were helping the street vendor clean up.

"Where'd you get these?" Nish asked, impressed.

"Found 'em on the street," Andy said.

Everyone laughed.

Everyone but Travis. This wasn't some rich hotel that "would never miss" a few lighters and chocolate bars; this was a real person trying to make a living. Travis was furious that Andy would do something like that to the vendor — who had *thanked* them, for heaven's sake.

Nish put the glasses on and checked himself out in a store window.

"Cool," he said. "Thanks."

Andy and Nish began walking down the street together, leaving the other three behind them.

Data and Gordie moved to catch up, swept up in the adventure, the fun, the *daring*.

Travis followed along, furious at himself for being there, for saying nothing.

He was a failure as a captain.

## 7

TRAVIS WONDERED HOW AIRPLANES COULD FLY. Not how they actually did it, but how they could land and take off in a wind like this. The tour guide said it was usually like this at the top of the CN Tower. It felt as if the wind was whipping the tower like the aerial on a car going through a car wash.

Nish had come up in the elevator, but he wasn't going back down that way. Halfway up the outside of the thin structure, he had made an announcement that almost panicked everyone packed into the glassed-in elevator.

"*I think I'm going to hurl!*"

But he didn't. He just turned a bit green and closed his eyes behind his stolen sunglasses and held his breath. When the elevator reached the top he went to the washroom and sat for a long time. Not sick, just gathering his courage.

Travis couldn't understand Nish's fear of heights. He remembered the time they went up White Mountain at Lake Placid and Nish had reacted the same way. Nish would block a shot with his teeth if he thought it would win the

Screech Owls a hockey game, but he wouldn't climb up on a garage roof even if he thought it would get him drafted into the NHL. He'd only stepped into the elevator because he couldn't stand the idea of them calling him a chicken.

Travis loved it. He loved the way he could look down and see SkyDome and the way he could look out over Lake Ontario all the way to the United States. A small commuter plane was coming in to land at the Island Airport, and already it was well below where Travis stood.

It had been Derek and Lars who'd come running from the far side of the circular observation deck to tell the rest of them about the wind. Standing where they were, they had been protected and hadn't felt the full force of the blow. But Lars – "Cherry" – had walked around and come upon it, gone back for his new friend Derek, and now the two of them had already mastered one of the greatest sensations Travis had ever felt: they could stand facing the wind, hold their arms out like an airplane, and fall forward – but never hit the ground.

The wind was cold this high up, but it didn't seem to bother them. It held them at a forty-five-degree angle, floating in outer space but for the contact of their shoes on the deck. It was fantastic: the wind pushing and falling, their bodies moving with the flow like weeds in a river. Only in their case, the flow was pushing them back up instead of ahead and down. It felt as if they had beaten gravity.

"*Amazing!*" Fahd shouted. They could barely hear him.

"*Get Nish!*" Gordie Griffith shouted.

Travis found Nish staring out through one of the coin-operated binoculars. It seemed he was more interested in having something to hang on to than to look through. Though it was cold up here, Nish was sweating heavily.

"You gotta see this," Travis said.

"I've seen enough," Nish answered. "I'm going back down."

"But you said you'd never get back on the elevator."

Nish looked desperate. "I'm going down the stairs."

"Stairs?"

"Yeah – over there."

Travis looked over toward an exit.

"I asked," Nish said. "People do it all the time. Willie says there's 1,760 steps, 138 separate landings."

"We haven't got time."

"Sure we do. Game's not till five-thirty."

Travis looked at his good friend. He could sense the terror in Nish's eyes. This was no time to push him further. If Nish saw what the wind was doing to his teammates on the other side of the deck, he'd pass out. He needed Travis now, and this was one time the captain wasn't going to let a teammate down.

"I'll see if anyone else wants to go."

They all thought it was a great idea. Travis presented the suggestion as a team project, something that would bring them all together. They'd "floated" together; now they could all say they'd walked down every step of the CN Tower together, all 1,760 of them. It would be like a souvenir.

They found Nish waiting at the stairway. He, too, was pretending there was more to this than merely giving him a way to avoid the glass elevator. He had his watch off and was holding it in his hand. He was setting up the stopwatch to time them.

"Everybody throws in a couple of bucks," said Nish. "First one to hit the bottom gets it all. No jumping allowed."

Everyone laughed at Nish's little joke. Nish seemed relieved. Relieved to be leaving the tower. Relieved not to be on the elevator. Relieved to have the company.

Travis had a sudden thought that, as captain, he probably should have told Muck or his father that they were walking down. But what would it matter? They were all supposed to meet at the entrance at one o'clock and then go for lunch. Everyone had to get down somehow.

"I'm in!" shouted Data.

"Me too," agreed Liz.

"And me."

"Travis'll hold the money," Nish said.

Travis found his hand filling with loonies and two-dollar bills. He took it all, counted it, and announced: "Thirty-four bucks." A lot of money to the winner. His first hope was that he would win himself, but that didn't seem fair since he was holding it. He was captain: he shouldn't win.

"Okay," Nish announced. "Wait'll I count down!"

They waited, pushing toward the door, each one jockeying for a better position.

"Three! . . . Two! . . . One! . . . Go!" Nish yelled.

They took off in a scramble, pushing, jostling, almost as if they were all atoms again, fighting for the puck in the same corner of the rink. Travis's first thought was that they'd made a mistake; someone was going to get hurt. But by the fourth turn in the staircase they had spread out, and all he could hear from above and below was shrieks of pleasure. What a great idea!

For a long time Travis kept count. By the mid-fifties, however, he was beginning to lose track of how many flights of stairs they had pounded down, whirling around each time to begin another. Fifty-three? Or was this fifty-four? What did it matter?

Somewhere in the eighties — he *thought* — Travis began to feel it. He had passed a number of players — Fahd, Liz, Willie — who had started fast but were now walking. Their legs were killing them. So were his. He felt as if his legs were another part of him, a borrowed part that might buckle any minute.

But he kept going. By the time he had passed maybe the hundredth flight, it had been some time since he had heard any shrieks of joy. There was the odd moan and yelp of pain, but no longer any sign of fun.

He knew he was nearing the bottom and kept going. He could hear voices — then a scream!

"Ooowwwwwwwwwwwwww!!"

He could hear more voices — all filled with concern. Travis hurried down three more flights and turned to find several of his teammates gathered around Nish, who was lying crumpled in the corner of the stairwell. Nish was moaning.

"What happened?" Travis called.

"He fell from the top step," Andy said. "I was right behind him."

Travis's first thought was: Did Andy push Nish? Were they racing? Of course they were racing — and Travis had the prize-money in his pocket to prove it!

He pushed through and knelt by Nish, who had tears in his eyes and was holding his leg.

"You okay?"

"I–think–I–broke–my–ankle," Nish answered through gritted teeth. He was in real pain.

"We're only four flights from the bottom," Wilson said.

"You better go down and tell somebody," Travis said. "We'll wait here – we better not move him."

"What're you going to do?" Nish asked nervously.

"They'll bring a stretcher up," said Travis. "You'll have to go to the hospital."

Nish's face seemed to take on a new agony.

"*I can't!*"

"What do you mean, '*can't*'? You'll have to if that's what they decide."

"But I can't, Trav," Nish said, looking around, lowering his voice to a whisper, "I haven't got any underwear on!"

Travis stared into the terrified face of his best friend. No underwear? He'd come with only the one pair and given up on them after the freezer incident. And he still hadn't gone shopping for some new ones.

"Nothing I can do about it," said Travis. Except, he felt like adding, *laugh*.

Nish's ankle wasn't broken, but it was twisted and swollen. They had taken him over to the Sick Children's Hospital on University Avenue. The X-Rays showed nothing was broken, but they'd wrapped the foot and outfitted him with crutches and given him instructions about icing. No one said anything to him about his lack of underwear.

Nish took it all very well. At least he was off the dreaded Tower. No one claimed the prize money, and Travis made sure everyone got their two dollars back. It now seemed like a dumb idea for them to have raced down.

Travis had watched while Barry, the assistant coach, broke the news to Muck, and he had noted how the coach listened and nodded and bounced on the balls of his feet as he did so – always a sure sign to the Screech Owls that Muck was upset. The quieter Muck went, the more it bothered them. Muck's silence was worse than if he'd lined them up at centre ice and screamed at them. Muck's silences didn't bother the ears – but they sure hurt.

## 8

TRAVIS FELT AS IF HE HAD OVERSTRETCHED ELASTICS in his legs instead of muscles. He could barely walk. He wasn't able to walk at all down stairs. Nor could any other of the Screech Owls – especially Nish, who wasn't even capable of hobbling in a straight line. Yet here they were, lining up for the face-off in Game Two of the Little Stanley Cup.

They needed to win this game. The Montreal Vedettes were one of the top teams in their division, and Muck and the coaches had expected it would be either the Vedettes or the Screech Owls in the final against the powerful Toronto Towers. The Owls' defence might have been a bit better than the Vedettes' – but better because of Nish, who was no longer able to play.

Travis knew they were in trouble long before the opening face-off. Muck had no speech for them – his silence still saying it all – and Mr. Dillinger had been quiet and frowning, which was most unusual for him. Nish had come in on his new crutches and sat in the dressing room to inspire the team, but it had inspired no one. All they could think about was how much they needed him and how sore their legs were from their foolish race down the CN Tower.

The puck dropped, and the big Vedettes centre took it easily from Derek and sent it back to his right defenceman. It was Travis's job to cut him off and take away the pass, if possible, but when he dug in to spring toward the defender, his legs felt like rubber.

The Vedettes' defenceman fired the puck across ice to his far winger, and when Travis turned, too late, the defender hit him with an elbow. It caught Travis on the side of the helmet and, with his legs already weakened, put him down instantly. He could hear the crowd yelling and his bench yelling, but there was no whistle. He couldn't get up, and the next thing he heard was the crowd cheering a Vedettes goal.

Travis got to his feet slowly, feeling terrible. First game, his line had scored immediately; second game, it had happened to them, with Travis lying face down on the ice at the time. He pushed his aching legs toward the bench, afraid even to look at his teammates. He could have sworn he heard the word "wimp" – from a teammate with a deep voice – but he wasn't sure. He pretended he hadn't heard it.

But Travis wasn't alone. By the time all three

44

lines had had their first shifts, it was obvious to everyone that no one on the Screech Owls had any jump. Not even Dmitri, whose entire game was his quick acceleration and speed. It was as if the Screech Owls were playing a player short – two players at times – the entire game.

At the end of the first period, they were down only 2–0 thanks to Jeremy Weathers' fine goal-tending. Dmitri finally did get a break in the second and scored to make it 2–1, but the Vedettes scored on an excellent two-on-one against Willie, who was filling in for Nish. Travis couldn't help but think that if it had been Nish back there, he would have had the pass.

In the third period, Travis could feel his legs beginning to come back. Dmitri had more jump as well. The Vedettes were just dumping the puck in, trying to kill off the clock, and Travis, feeling finally that he was in the game, raced back to pick the puck up behind his own net. He hit Derek as he curled back with a pass at the blueline and, without even looking, Derek fed the puck between his own legs to Dmitri, who was already in full flight.

Dmitri blew past the defenceman who should have been watching him. He kept to the boards, hoping to sweep in across net – his favourite play – and get the goaltender moving just before he put it on the short side. But the opposite defenceman came hurling toward Dmitri, completely ignoring the open ice on the other side.

Travis saw his chance and shot for it as fast as his weakened legs would take him. Normally, he would have already been up with Dmitri, but he was still in the centre-ice zone when Dmitri flicked the puck back. It was a beautiful play, one that only Dmitri, or Sarah Cuthbertson last year, could have made. The puck floated through the air and then landed flat, slowing instantly. A location pass, placed perfectly where a player is going to be rather than where a player is at the moment of the pass.

Travis drove hard toward the net and picked up the puck as it lay there waiting for him, just inside the blueline. He came in alone, the defenceman committed to Dmitri and now entirely out of the play. Travis dropped his shoulder and the Vedettes' goaltender went down on the fake. Travis went to his backhand and hoisted as high as he could. The puck pinged off the crossbar and went high over the glass into the crowd. What he couldn't do in the warm-up he had done in the game. But now it meant nothing. There was no time left for the Screech Owls.

"We'll walk back to the hotel, okay?" Muck said after the game. The team groaned as one.

"All except Nish, who'll ride with Barry. The

rest of you can use the exercise. Fortunately for you, it's mostly downhill."

*Downhill!*

Muck never even smiled – but he knew, he knew.

## 9

EVERYBODY'S LEGS FELT BETTER THE FOLLOWING morning. Even Nish's injured ankle. He hobbled to the bathroom, no crutches, and even tried putting his weight down on it. But it still hurt. He was pushing it too soon.

Travis was first dressed and out the door for breakfast, and first, therefore, to notice the Eaton's bag hanging off the outside of the doorhandle. He took it off and looked inside: three brand-new pairs of youth underwear, large, still in their package.

Travis turned and fired the bag at Nish, who was sitting on the side of the bed. Nish caught it, opened it, and pulled out the package of new underwear as if he held the winning ticket in a draw.

"Good old Mr. Dillinger!" he shouted.

"How do you know it was him?" Travis asked.

"He was with me in emergency – he was there when they cut away my jeans."

Data stared, unbelieving. "They cut off your pants?"

"Yeah, of course – they could hardly pull them off over my foot, could they?"

"Who was 'they'?" Data wanted to know.

"A nurse. Who else?"

"She cut your jeans off and you had nothing on underneath?"

Nish was turning red. "I had a towel Mr. Dillinger gave me."

"*A towel?*" Willie screeched.

"Yeah – so what?"

"Maybe she thought you were a dancer from the Zanzibar," said Data.

Everyone laughed. Everyone except Nish, who was struggling with the plastic to get the bag opened and the new underwear on.

Mr. Dillinger had arranged for the entire team to visit the Hockey Hall of Fame. The visit, even more than the tournament, had been the talk of the Screech Owls since they began their bottle drives and bingo games and sponsorship search to fund their trip. Many of the parents were also going, and were just as excited as the players.

The Hall of Fame staff were expecting them, and had even laid on a wheelchair for Nish, who sat down on it as if he were royalty taking the throne. He even snapped his fingers for Travis to start pushing, which Travis did while everyone cheered and laughed.

Most of them shot right through the historical stuff and headed for the broadcast area, where they'd be able to broadcast their own games into microphones. Travis had to push Nish and so he was slowed down, and very soon glad that he had been, for the history section was wonderful.

There were old sweaters and old skates, sticks made of a single piece of wood, and wonderful old photographs that seemed to say that everything imaginable has changed about this wonderful game, but also that nothing whatsoever has changed.

Together, Travis and Nish looked at all the glass cases containing the stories of the truly great. Howie Morenz. Aurel Joliat. King Clancy. Jean Béliveau. Gordie Howe. Bobby Orr.

"Look at this!" Nish shouted.

He had wheeled himself over to the Maurice "Rocket" Richard exhibit and was pointing to Richard's stick as if it were the biggest joke in the world.

"'*Love & Bennett Limited*'!" Nish laughed. "*That's* a stick manufacturer? He used a Love & Bennett instead of an Easton or a Sherwood – I don't believe it. And just look at it: absolutely perfectly straight. How the heck could you even take a shot with it?"

Travis stood staring at the Richard exhibit for a long time. Richard had once scored fifty goals in fifty games. He had often heard his grandfather say that half the goals from the old days could never be scored these days because no one in hockey knew how to take a backhander any more. He claimed it was physically impossible to take a proper backhander with a curved blade.

"Ah, now *there's* a hockey stick!" Nish announced.

He was pointing to one of Bobby Hull's. It didn't even resemble a stick. It was so curved it looked like the letter "J."

"That can't be real," said Travis.

"Sure – you could do anything you wanted before they made them illegal," said Nish. He shook his head in admiration. "Those were the good old days."

The two boys moved on. Past the international hockey stuff, past the broadcast zone, where they could hear Data and Fahd high above them screeching out play-by-play into a microphone, past the minivan with dummies in the seats and hockey equipment stashed in the back, past the display of goaltender masks.

They stopped at the Coca-Cola rink, where several of the Screech Owls were taking shots and having their speed measured by radar. Wilson was just about to shoot.

"It doesn't give minus signs!" Nish yelled out.

Wilson stopped, laughing. "You're throwing me off!" he shouted.

"The only way they'd ever time your shot is with a sun dial!" Nish shot back. He had returned to form. Travis could only laugh and push on.

In the replica of the Montreal Canadiens' dressing room, they found Jennie and Jeremy sitting beside a pair of goaltender pads and a big sweater on a hanger: No. 29, Ken Dryden's.

"You think if you sit there long enough something might rub off?" Nish asked.

"We think if we sit here long enough you might go away," said Jennie.

"Let's get outta here," Nish ordered. He snapped his fingers and pointed toward the exit. Travis, his servant, pushed on, trying not to laugh out loud.

"I want to see the Stanley Cup," Nish said.

"I think it's upstairs."

"That's your problem, not mine."

## 10

TRAVIS WOULD HAVE TO FIND AN ELEVATOR.

There was no other way to get Nish up to the next floor to the Great Hall where they kept all the NHL trophies, including the Stanley Cup.

He asked one of the custodians for directions. There was an elevator at the rear, she told him. It was for the staff to come and go from their offices on the third and fourth floors, but it was also available for the use of anyone in need – and his friend in the wheelchair was certainly in need.

Travis pushed Nish down a long corridor, at the end of which were sliding doors and a single button. Travis pushed the button and the doors opened on an empty elevator.

"Lingerie, please." Nish announced, as if he were addressing an elevator operator in a department store.

"You're sick," Travis said.

Nish grinned: "And proud of it."

They rose to the second floor and the doors began to open.

Suddenly, both were blinded by a flash of light!

At first Travis couldn't see, but as the flash

faded from his eyes he could make out two bulky figures, one with a camera half-hidden in his opened coat.

The men seemed caught off guard. The man taking the pictures – dark, surly, with a scar down the side of his face as if he'd run into a skate – seemed to be trying to hide the camera. The other – tall, balding, but with a ponytail tied behind his head – seemed nervous.

"How ya doin', boys?" the tall man asked.

"Okay," Travis answered, unsure.

"We're just taking some shots for a few renovations," the man explained.

Travis pushed Nish past. It didn't make any sense. The Hockey Hall of Fame was almost brand new. Why would it need fixing up already?

"What the heck's with them?" Nish asked as they moved further down the corridor.

"I have no idea," said Travis.

When they got to the Great Hall where the trophies were – a dazzle of lights on silver and glass, the Norris, the Calder, the Lady Byng, the Hart, the Vezina – several of the Screech Owls were already positioned in the designated area for taking their own photographs.

The scene made Travis even more suspicious of the men. If they had come in here with a camera, surely it was for this. Why would they want to take a picture of an elevator?

"*There's the Stanley Cup!*" Nish shouted, pointing.

Derek and Willie were already there. The cup looked glorious. So shining, so rich, so remarkably *familiar*, even though none of them had ever seen it in real life before this moment.

"This isn't the real one," said Willie, who knew everything.

"Whadya mean?" Nish scowled, disbelieving.

Willie pointed back over his shoulder. "The real one, the original one that Lord Stanley gave back in 1893, is back over there in the vault. This building used to be a bank, you know. They keep it back there because it's considered too fragile to present to the players, so they present this one – which in a way makes this one the real Stanley Cup as well."

Travis looked to see what Willie was talking about. He could see another room back behind huge steel doors – "LORD STANLEY'S VAULT," the sign overhead said. There were more lights in there and what appeared to be another, smaller trophy.

*And the two men were there, too!*

The shorter, dark one had his camera out again. He was flashing pictures as fast as he could. But not of the cup, of everything else: the walls, the vault doors, the base the trophy stood on.

What were they up to?

"Wait here," Travis said to Nish.

Nish turned back, hardly caring. He could get Data to push him if necessary. But anyway he wasn't much interested in leaving the cup he was planning to carry around Maple Leaf Gardens.

Travis circled wide around the other trophies so he could come up on the entrance to the smaller room without being seen.

There was no one in the vault but the two men, still taking photographs. It made no sense.

Travis kept close to the wall and edged to the doorway. He could hear the taller man talking.

"It's perfect," he kept saying. "Perfect."

"No one can see from any of the other areas. There's only the one surveillance camera, the main alarm, and a secondary alarm on the display case. We plan it right and we can be in and out of here in less than thirty minutes."

The man with the camera stopped and turned, scowling.

"Keep it down. You wanna tell the whole country?"

The tall one laughed. "The whole country will know soon enough – and they'll pay whatever it takes to get this baby back, believe me."

Travis could feel his legs shaking, and it wasn't from the CN Tower run.

## 11

TRAVIS HURRIED BACK TO THE GROUP AROUND THE other Stanley Cup. They were taking so many pictures and talking so loudly that he couldn't get a word in edgewise. But even if he could, what would he say? That there were two men over there plotting to steal the real Stanley Cup? What if someone pointed? What if the men called him a liar? What if he ended up in trouble just trying to alert someone? He would tell Muck; Muck would know what to do.

The custodians of the trophy room asked the Screech Owls if they would mind moving on to let some of the other visitors closer. Travis was happy to leave – it would give him a chance to get to Muck before the two thieves left the building. Muck would tell the security people and they'd know how to stop them.

"Let's go back down to the souvenir shop," Travis suggested.

"Yeah, let's," Derek agreed.

They had all seen the store as they'd come in, and all had vowed to get back in time to buy something to remember their visit by.

"I need a T-shirt," Nish said. He always had to have a souvenir T-shirt from every tournament. Always.

"Maybe they sell Hall of Fame underwear," Willie suggested, to great laughter from the rest.

"Very funny," said Nish. "Now push."

Travis saw Muck as the coach came out of the Hall of Fame's store. He and Nish had just dropped off the wheelchair, thanked the workers for it, and Travis was helping Nish, who was back on his crutches, out through the turnstiles. He could tell from a distance that Muck was not at all pleased.

Muck was standing with two of the Hall of Fame's security guards and a man in a suit who looked like he ran the place. They were all deep in conversation. One of the security people had her arms full of merchandise.

They drew closer, and Nish saw Andy over by the cash register. He looked shaken. He was with Lars and Jesse and Liz, and they all looked upset.

"What's up?" Nish said as he hobbled up to them.

"Something to do with Data and Wilson and Fahd," said Liz. "They've got them back in that office there."

Travis could just make out Data's head

through the window in the office door. He looked as if he was crying.

"They got caught lifting," said Andy.

Travis turned. "*What?*"

"They had some T-shirts stuffed into their windbreakers."

Travis couldn't believe what he was hearing. *Caught stealing?* Data? Wilson? Fahd? They wouldn't steal – *would they?*

"You gotta be kidding," said Nish.

"I'm not," said Andy. "I was right here when they got picked up."

Yeah, Travis wanted to say, right here leading them on.

"Why would they do it?" Nish asked.

Andy had no answer. Because he knew? Travis wondered. Or because there was no answer?

"There must be some mistake," Travis said. "They wouldn't steal."

Andy gave Travis his sarcastic lifted-eyebrow look. "Yeah, right," he said.

They *had* been stealing. The cameras had caught it all, and they were found with the goods stuffed into their windbreakers. That was what the security woman had been holding.

Muck and Mr. Dillinger and Travis's dad had then met alone with the man in the suit. After a long time, the three men came over to where Data, Fahd, and Wilson had gone to wait with the assistant coaches. Muck and Mr. Lindsay did the talking. Fahd was wiping away more tears. Wilson was sniffing.

The three boys got up and left with Mr. Lindsay and Barry. Muck came over, limping slightly from his old hockey injury. He signalled the rest of the team to follow him to a quiet corner.

"Sit down," Muck said. They sat. Some on benches. Some on the floor.

Muck took his time. Whether it was for effect or because he didn't know what to say, Travis didn't know, but Muck had a look that he had seen only a few times in the past. And Travis didn't like it.

"You're not stupid people," Muck said. "Though some of you, it seems, can still act stupid. I don't need to tell you what happened."

He paused again.

"The manager had some good advice for our three teammates," he continued. "He recommended they go home and tell their parents what they've done and what they think about what they've done. He said if they promised him that they would do this, he wouldn't be pressing charges. The three young men are on their way home as we speak. Mr. Lindsay is driving them.

"They are no longer members of the Screech Owls."

Nish couldn't help himself: "*Forever?*"

"For as long as it takes," Muck answered.

No one had a clue what he meant. And no one had the nerve to ask.

"Let's go back to the hotel now," Muck said, and he turned to go.

Travis didn't know what to do. How could he now chase after Muck with a story that two men were planning to steal the Stanley Cup? Why would Muck believe him or anyone else on the Screech Owls after what had happened? Nothing like this ever happened when Sarah had been captain.

And now he couldn't even tell his father, who had left without a word to take the three disgraced players home. Given the distance, he probably wouldn't be back.

"Give me a hand, eh?" Nish said, trying to get up. Travis helped his friend to his feet and bent down for his crutches. As he stood up and handed them to Nish, he saw the two men come up the stairs from the Hall of Fame and out the door.

They were *leaving*. Heading off, Travis was certain, to put the finishing touches to their plan.

## 12

TRAVIS HAD NEVER FELT SO YOUNG AND INSIGNIFI-
cant in all his life. He had gone to the hotel pay-
phones and, with two quarters, made two calls.
The first was to the Hockey Hall of Fame, the
second to the police.

"Two men are going to steal the Stanley Cup,"
he'd said, wishing his voice didn't sound so young.

"Is that right?" a man at the Hall of Fame had
said.

"Yes."

"Well, we watch it pretty closely," the man
said. "What's your name, son?"

He couldn't give it. The last thing Travis
wanted was the police and the Hall of Fame security people racing to the hotel to talk to Muck
about what a Screech Owl knew about some plot
to steal the Stanley Cup. That would be the last
straw for Muck. He might pull the entire team
out of the Little Stanley Cup. And Travis, as
captain, would never be forgiven by his teammates for such a thing. So far, he hadn't even told
Nish what he knew – or at least suspected. Nish
could never keep his mouth shut, and Travis

didn't want the whole team knowing. Not until he'd figured out what to do.

"They *really* are!" Travis insisted. He knew he sounded like a silly fool. "I heard them plotting to do it."

"Yes," the man said. He sounded bored, as if he handled several such calls a day. "Well, if we don't know who you are, then we don't know whether to believe you, do we?"

Travis had hung up. Both times. His call to the police was almost exactly the same. Both were utter failures. They thought he was a kid pulling a prank.

Travis gave up. If the Stanley Cup was stolen, so be it – he had tried his best. At least he told himself it was his best.

But he knew it wasn't.

To no one's surprise, Muck cancelled the trip to the Leafs game that night. A once-in-a-lifetime opportunity lost because three of the team got caught shoplifting. There were bad feelings all round. Most were angry with the three boys for costing them a chance to see a real NHL game at Maple Leaf Gardens. Travis was angry with Andy Higgins, even though he had no proof that Andy had been involved or had put the three up to stealing. He just knew Andy was in there somewhere.

Muck put a 9:30 curfew on the team and did room checks to make sure everyone was where they should be and ready for bed. With Data now back home, Travis moved over into the other bed with Willie so Nish and his injured ankle could have a bed to themselves.

At 8:00 a.m. the Screech Owls were scheduled to play the Muskoka Wildlife – an all-star team made up of players from the three towns in the Ontario resort area – and the winner of the game would have an outside chance of making the final. It all depended on what happened in the Toronto Towers' next game against the Sudbury Nickel Belts, a team both the Owls and Towers had beaten several times. If somehow Sudbury could beat the Towers, then the Owls would still have an outside chance.

Nish said his ankle was feeling much better. He used only one crutch to go down for breakfast, and by the time they got to the arena he was claiming he was good enough to play.

Muck didn't think so. But he was three defencemen short, with Nish's ankle and Data and Willie sent home. Gordie Griffith had already been told to play defence, with Liz moving over to centre the second line and Travis double-shifted to cover the shortage at left wing. Muck said Nish could go out for the warm-up, but he wouldn't make any decision until they were ready to start the game.

Travis felt great. His legs were back. He hit the crossbar with his very first warm-up shot. His skates were sharp and he had no sense of them being on his feet – the best possible feeling for a good skater. He was sure he was finally going to have a good game and glad that he would be getting extra ice time.

Nish tried, but couldn't do it. He could barely take his corners.

"Not this game," Muck told him. "You'd better get undressed."

"Can't I just sit on the bench?" Nish asked.

Muck stared at him, then nodded. Nish would at least make it *look* as if the Screech Owls had enough players.

The Muskoka Wildlife were good. They had excellent skaters, good shooters, and big players. Travis and some of the other Owls found them intimidating just to watch in the warm-up, but Muck said something just before the face-off that made them think they might have a chance.

He called them all around the bench while the Wildlife were down in their own end going through their team yell.

"All-star teams are rarely good teams," Muck said, seeming to contradict himself. "You put three stars together, you don't necessarily have a line. You have a situation where everyone is chasing glory, you won't have anyone chasing the puck. Understand?"

They all shouted that they did, but Travis wasn't so sure any of them followed Muck when he talked this way. He knew the reason his line worked was because Dmitri had the speed, Derek could make the passes, and he, Travis, could come up with the puck. A line of three Dmitris might look sensational, but who was going to dig out the puck for them?

Five minutes into the game, the Muskoka Wildlife were up 2–0 on the Screech Owls. Muck's little speech was starting to ring a bit hollow, but he wasn't letting up. "Two goals on two individual rushes," he told them. "You stop the individual, you stop this whole team."

Muck changed the game plan so that there were two Screech Owls going in to forecheck instead of the Owls' usual plan of having one go in and the other two forwards holding back. Muck's hunch was that the Wildlife would be weakest on passing because each all-star player would always be trying to make the big play.

He was right. The first time Travis and Dmitri pressed in on a defender, he tried to step around them. He got past Dmitri, but Travis took the body, forcing the defenceman to panic and dump the puck out blind. Derek snared it at the blue-line with his glove, dropped the puck, and hit Dmitri as he circled the Muskoka net. Dmitri waited for the goaltender to make his move – and he did, going down – and then roofed a forehand into the top of the net. The Owls were back in the game.

Not long into the second period "Cherry" Johanssen hit Liz Moscovitz with a breakaway pass and Liz was home free from centre ice in, the Owls all standing at the bench, petrified she would blow it. Liz had speed, but bad luck in scoring. "Stone hands," she said herself. But this time it seemed she had Dmitri's hands, deking out the Muskoka goaltender and dropping a light backhand in behind him. Tie game.

Once the game had been tied, Muck's words came true. The Muskoka Wildlife gave up even pretending to pass and work as a team and turned instead to an endless series of individual efforts. All the Owls had to do was concentrate on the puck carrier and there would be a turnover and the Screech Owls could counterattack.

Cherry Johanssen used his speed to pick up a dropped puck and rushed down the ice with Derek and Travis. They crossed the blueline on a three-on-one, Cherry slipped it under the defenceman's stick to Derek, and Derek dropped it back to Travis, who faked a shot and slid the puck over to Cherry, who had the wide open net to score.

The Screech Owls had a 3–2 lead. The Wildlife tried frantically to come back, but Jennie never even let a rebound out. The Owls had won the game they had to win.

When the horn blew, the Screech Owls bolted over the boards and the entire team spilled over the ice toward Jennie as if they'd been dumped from a pail. Nish, of course, was right in the middle of it all. The only player on the team who hadn't broken a sweat.

They lined up for the naming of the Player of the Game. When the announcer began, "Most Valuable Player, Screech Owls . . . ," Nish pushed out from the blueline to the centre of the ice and did a little twirl. The Muskoka Wildlife, who weren't paying full attention, rapped their sticks on the ice to congratulate him while his own team booed. ". . . is the goaltender, *Jennie Staples!*"

Now the Owls could cheer and slam their sticks. Jennie skated out and collected her prize, a tournament T-shirt. As she skated back she rolled it up and tossed it at Nish, who caught it, delighted.

"Take it," she said. "You earned it."

"How so?" Nish asked.

"First game you ever dressed for when you haven't screened me," Jennie laughed.

"It's not 'screening,'" he protested, "it's *blocking.*"

"Whatever," Jennie said. "It's still your big ugly butt in my face."

## 13

"YOU COME WITH ME," NISH SAID TO TRAVIS.

Nish had come up to him in the hotel lobby and told him he had been thinking about the sunglasses and what to do with them.

"You should have taken them back right when Andy handed them to you."

"I didn't, okay. And I can't give them back now."

Travis didn't suppose Nish could. How would it look: Nish, nearly two days later, handing over something and saying it must have landed in his pocket when he dumped the vendor's table?

"But I can *put* them back," Nish said, smiling.

"What do you mean?"

"If Andy can lift them, I can lift them back, don't you think? I'll just have to make sure I don't get caught."

"You're going to sneak them back?"

"Reverse shoplifting. Like a film running backwards. C'mon!"

The two of them, alone, started off down Yonge Street. The springlike weather was hold-ing. Nish wanted to try walking without the crutches, and he seemed fine except for a slight limp.

They walked down the other side this time until they were past the Zanzibar strip club – Nish had good reason to steer clear of it – and then, a half-block below, they crossed back over.

Nish had the stolen sunglasses in his pocket. When they reached the vendor's table he began trying on various glasses and twice asked the vendor for the little hand-held mirror so he could see what they looked like. They all looked ridiculous.

Travis moved on down the street to wait. He was uncomfortable standing there and knew that two young kids would make the vendor suspicious, especially if they weren't buying anything.

As he was waiting, two familiar faces cut through the crowd outside the Zanzibar. He knew them both immediately – one tall and balding with a ponytail, the other dark with a nasty scar on the face. It was the two crooks from the Hockey Hall of Fame!

They came to a stop right beside Travis, not because they recognized him, but because they were hungry. When Travis turned his back so they wouldn't recognize him, he saw was standing right next to a hot-dog vendor, and that was where the two plotters had been headed. They ordered bratwurst and Cokes, and while they were waiting for the vendor to finish cooking the big sausages, they talked.

"You're certain we can trust him?" the short dark one asked.

"For five thousand dollars you can trust anyone."

"He leaves the fire exit open – that's what he said, eh – after six p.m.?"

"That's when they close today. There'll be just the two security guards after that – and one of them's one of us." The one with the ponytail laughed, enjoying his little secret.

The two plotters finished their food and drinks and were off down Yonge Street. Travis shifted carefully as they passed, always keeping his face out of sight, and when they were gone he let out his breath as if he were letting a balloon go.

Nish came running up.

"Done! He never even noticed."

"Good," said Travis. "But now we've got another problem."

## 14

MOST OF THE SCREECH OWLS WERE GATHERED IN the lobby when Travis and Nish returned from their mission to return the stolen sunglasses. Liz raced toward them with the news.

"The Towers lost!"

"*What?*" Nish couldn't believe what he was hearing.

"You're kidding," Travis said.

"No, I'm not. They ran into a really hot goal-tender and lost 3–2. It came down to total goals – and we're in!"

"*Fan–tas–tic!!*" shouted Nish.

The rest of the team – what was left of it, anyway – came running over to tell Nish and Travis, even though they obviously already knew. Travis could feel the excitement in his teammates, Gordie, Jennie, Willie, Jesse, all of them shouting his and Nish's name. Then he caught sight of Andy Higgins along the far wall, just staring. Travis couldn't tell what Andy's stare meant. Resentment over the excitement everyone else was showing toward Travis and Nish? Jealousy? Or just that he didn't feel a full part of the Screech Owls yet?

Travis saw Muck and the assistants coming in through the hotel's revolving doors and went over. Muck showed no emotion.

"Well," he said. "I guess we got in the back door."

Travis was startled at the contrast between his teammates and his coaches. The team had all been celebrating; the coaches, particularly Muck, looked as if they'd just come from a funeral.

Travis didn't have to have it spelled out for him. Muck had been embarrassed and humiliated by the incident at the Hockey Hall of Fame. It didn't matter that Muck himself had nothing to do with what had happened – in the coach's eyes he had everything to do with it. A team wasn't made up of individuals, just as he'd said when they played the Muskoka Wildlife; if the Screech Owls were a real team, then what some of them did affected them all. And whatever the team did, both on and off the ice, reflected on the coach.

Travis felt just as disappointed himself. He didn't feel excited like his teammates. He felt empty.

The final was scheduled for the next day at 11:00 a.m. Muck put them through an afternoon practice, and they all worked hard. Nish skated and even played a little scrimmage, but still wasn't fully recovered. The rest were sharp and eager, which seemed to please Muck. He didn't cancel the planned visit to the Ontario Science Centre as he had the Leafs game.

It was a difficult afternoon for Travis. He did laugh once, when the Science Centre guide selected Nish to stand on a rubber mat and put his hand on a silver globe while they shot a charge of static electricity through him. Nish's hair looked like it was trying to run away from him! But there was a big difference between laughing at a little moment and feeling good about their whole time in Toronto.

They went to the Science Centre cafeteria for a snack at the end, and Muck asked Travis to come and sit with him. Muck had two Cokes, one for each of them.

Travis felt his stomach churning. He didn't know what Muck wanted. He didn't know what to say. Maybe he'd get a chance to talk about the two plotters.

Muck took a long drink of his Coke, swallowed, and stared hard at Travis.

"Did you know anything about the stealing?" he asked.

Travis shook his head. He knew Muck was talking about the Hockey Hall of Fame, and he had known nothing about it. But he did know about the other stealing, only it had involved others, not the three who were sent home, and Travis couldn't tell on Andy and Nish. He couldn't squeal. Certainly not on his best friend.

Technically, he was right to shake his head. But he was wrong, too. Either way, he was behaving like a wimp. A wimp if he squealed. A wimp by letting Muck think something was true when it wasn't exactly true.

"A good captain has to lead by example, Travis," Muck said. "I wanted you as captain for precisely that reason."

Travis swallowed hard. "Yes, sir."

Surprisingly, Muck gave a slight grin. "Think we can win with half a bench?"

Travis was relieved at the change of topic. "I hope so," he said.

Muck took another swallow, nodding.

"We don't deserve to," he said.

Muck gave them a free evening. He set the rules when they got back to the hotel lobby: "Stay in groups of a minimum of three. Stay off the streets, except for those who plan to go shopping at the Eaton Centre. Be in your rooms, lights out, by nine-thirty. I'll be checking."

Some of the Owls were going shopping with their parents. Some wanted to stay around the pool.

Travis was in the elevator when he decided to act. He and Nish were headed up to their rooms to change into their swimsuits, not knowing what else to do. Travis figured that, as captain and assistant captain, it was clear what their duty was.

All he could think about was Muck's enormous disappointment in the team and how a captain was expected to lead by example. Perhaps if he could prevent one of the thefts – a much bigger one than the lighters or sunglasses or T-shirts – he could be a good example, at least in his own eyes. That might be a start, anyway.

The elevator was just coming to a halt on their floor.

"Let's go back to the Hall of Fame," he said.

"Been there, done that," said Nish, unimpressed.

Travis made the decision he'd been avoiding. He had to tell Nish.

"We have to go back."

"What d'ya mean?"

"There's two guys planning to steal the Stanley Cup tonight."

Nish turned, staring. If his hair could have shot straight up without static electricity, it would have.

Good old Nish. Once Travis had explained, he was all for it, almost like a player who's been sitting on the bench all along and finally gets a chance to play. He understood why Travis had been unable to tell Muck. He was outraged that the police, as well as the Hall of Fame, had dismissed Travis as a childish prankster when he'd called. He saw this as a marvellous opportunity for them, supposedly the team leaders, to right a few wrongs. He had put back the sunglasses, and now he'd make sure the Stanley Cup never got lifted by anyone who wasn't on a winning team.

They prepared carefully. Nish had his little backpack, and they had apples and chocolate bars and drinking boxes to put in it.

"I hate those stupid boxes," said Nish.

"So do I, but pop cans make noise."

"Right."

"Do you have any shin-pad tape?" Travis asked.

"A couple rolls."

"Get them. You never know, they might come in handy."

"How'll we get there?" Nish asked.

"I've got subway tokens. It'll take us twenty minutes, tops."

Nish suddenly frowned: "We can't go."

"What do you mean?"

"Muck says we have to stick in threes."

Nish was right. They were already risking enough trouble just in going. But they might not even get out the front door of the hotel if they were on their own. More important, even if they did manage to slip away unnoticed, they were still only two peewee hockey players against two

grown crooks. They could use at least a third
person – if only to serve as lookout.

"We'd better find someone," Nish said.

"Data would be perfect."

"Data's probably been sent to his room until
the end of the next century."

"Derek?"

Nish shook his head. "Went to the movies."

They were stuck. Willie, their roommate, was
down in the pool. Besides, they needed Willie
here if they blew curfew. They'd left a note on
Willie's pillow telling him they might be a bit late
and to answer for them if Muck happened to
knock on the door.

They went down to the lobby, looking and
checking around. Everyone was either gone or
else tied up with plans.

All except one.

"Andy," Nish said. "He's not with anybody."

"Take a thief to catch a thief?" Travis asked,
incredulous.

"Why not?" Nish grinned. "He already thinks
like them."

Andy was sulking around the lobby. Since the
three shoplifters had been sent home, he'd been
more or less frozen out by the rest of the team.

Travis shrugged.

Nish headed toward Andy and Travis followed, feeling he really had no choice. Andy saw
them coming. He was sitting on one of the big

lobby chesterfields and had a plastic shopping bag on his lap. He shifted uncomfortably.

"What're you doing?" Nish asked, plunking down beside Andy.

"Nothin'," Andy replied. He seemed nervous.

"What's in the bag?" Nish asked. Good old Nish. Never shy about things.

"Nothin'."

"C'mon, let me see."

Nish grabbed the bag out of Andy's hands and dumped the contents out. The CN Tower lighters and the Blue Jays mug and the deck of cards came spilling out, as well as several loonies. As quick as he had dumped them out, Nish scooped everything back into the bag and threw it in Andy's lap.

Travis's first thought was that Andy had been stealing again from the shop. But why the loonies?

"I was trying to figure out how to get it back," Andy said.

"What's the money for?"

"To pay for the cigarettes, I guess. Whatever."

Nish was grinning: "Why the change of heart?"

"It's my fault they got caught, obviously." He stared hard at Travis. "You don't have to pretend everyone isn't blaming me for what happened."

Travis said nothing. What was there to say to Andy?

"I'll put it back for you," Nish said.

Andy looked at Nish, not understanding.

"I am the world's leading expert at returning stolen merchandise," Nish announced with pride. "Just give it to me."

Andy handed over the bag. Without a word, Nish got up and walked straight over into the gift shop. As casual as could be, Nish began talking with the old woman at the cash register and pointing to a cap clipped to a rack high above the front window. She nodded, got a short stool and a stick with a hook on it, and began reaching for the cap.

With the woman's back turned, Nish simply leaned over and stuffed the bag in one of the low shelves full of candy. She'd find it soon enough, but never figure it out.

She lowered the cap and handed it to an angelic-looking Nish, who tried it on, looked at his reflection in the window, and then, seeming disappointed, handed it back to the old woman. She nodded and turned to replace the cap. Nish walked out.

When he got back to where the others were waiting, he said, looking at Andy, "Travis, I think we've got our third man."

Travis found himself nodding.

## 15

THEY TOOK THE SUBWAY DOWN AND, WITH THEIR car fairly empty, explained all to Andy along the way. Travis couldn't believe the change in Andy. No longer surly, no longer staring at Travis as if there were some mysterious grudge between them. He seemed as keen as Nish to stop the heist of the Stanley Cup. He seemed proud to be part of the team that was setting out to save the cup.

Travis tried to figure it out. Maybe it all had to do with wanting to fit in instead of being different. Andy wasn't a good enough player that he'd make an impression on the other Screech Owls by his play alone. The team automatically loved Dmitri because he scored the goals, but for third-line players like Andy, it was different.

Andy had brought attention to himself with the shoplifting. He'd even been, momentarily, popular because of it. But now three of the players had been sent home for stealing and Andy had become a virtual outcast from the team.

They paid to go in. "We close in less than an hour," the young woman taking their money had said, but they had nodded and thanked her and happily paid the admission.

Travis kept looking at the various security guards, wondering which one was on the take for the five thousand dollars. The crooked security guard made it impossible for the boys to go to one of them and say that there was about to be a break-in. If they happened to pick the wrong one – and there weren't many to choose from – they would either blow their plan or, even worse, end up being taken hostage.

There was nothing to do but wait.

Travis felt a deep, deep shiver go through his body when the announcement came that the Hockey Hall of Fame was closing at 6:00 p.m. and visitors were to begin to leave. He knew now that it was just a matter of minutes. He also knew that in many ways these were the most crucial minutes. If they got kicked out, they wouldn't be able to do anything to prevent the theft.

The boys were concerned that the Hall of Fame might have taken a body count of all those entering and leaving. But Nish had already thought of this and, just for safety, had triggered the exit turnstiles three times as Travis was paying. If there was a counter, then the three boys would be cancelled out the moment they entered.

Travis couldn't believe the change in Andy. He'd suddenly come to life. Travis's idea had been for them to hide in the washroom while they closed the building. They could shut the doors and stand on the toilet seats and no one would see them.

"But they'd see closed doors and wonder," Andy cautioned. He was right.

And after they looked around, Andy had a better idea.

"Come on over here," he whispered just before the final closing announcement came.

They followed Andy to the minivan that was supposed to show a typical suburban hockey family of the 1990s. In the back was a hockey bag as high as the window, sticks stuffed in every which way, and in the seats up front the "family" was happily driving: dummy dad, dummy mom, dummy kids.

"Data's dad has one exactly the same," said Nish. "Right down to the little dummy in the back."

"We could crawl in here and wait them out," Andy said.

An excellent idea. Good for Andy, Travis thought, even though he shuddered slightly at the idea that he'd be in the pitch dark. No night light for him here. But this was much better than hoping to pass unnoticed in the washrooms. How would someone react, pushing open a door and seeing Nish standing on the lid?

Nish hurried over and carefully tried the

latch.It clicked and gave. He quickly checked to see if any of the custodians were watching, but there was no one. He lifted up the tailgate.

"Hey, Data," Nish said to the closest dummy kid. "Looking good, man. Looking good."

The boys scrambled in underneath the hockey equipment. Andy pulled down the tailgate so the roof light inside went out but the lock didn't catch. Getting back out would be a simple matter of pushing out from the bottom.

They settled down and everything went quiet. Travis could see out of the tinted glass even if he was at the far side of the trunk. He was pretty sure no one could see in.

"How long do we have to wait?" Andy asked.

"Not long," said Travis. "The security guard's supposed to rig the fire exit for them so they can come in without setting off the alarm."

"What if I have to go to the can?" Nish asked.

"Tough," said Travis. Then he giggled: "You should have brought extra underwear."

"Very funny," Nish said.

## 16

TRAVIS CHECKED HIS WATCH: 6:44 P.M. THE HOCKEY Hall of Fame was dark but hardly pitch black. He was grateful for the dim glow of the security lights. It was so silent he thought he could hear his heart beating.

They'd eaten their food and drunk the fruit juice. And then they had waited.

"*Ssshhhh!*"

It was Andy, who'd been on lookout. He ducked down below the windows. "Someone's coming with a flashlight!"

Travis stretched up, careful not to put his face too close to the tinted glass. He barely peeked out – he felt like a frog in water, with just his eyeballs showing – and could see the swinging wash of a flashlight along the hallway.

The beam turned full into the large room where the minivan sat. Travis instinctively ducked as it swept over the van. The light moved closer. Travis could sense Nish bobbing up to see, and he put his hand on his head and pushed down.

The beam turned and washed back over the robber with the ponytail.

"The elevator's over this way!" said another voice. It was like a hiss. But Travis could still recognize it. The smaller, darker one with the scar.

"Hold your horses," the ponytail told him. "We've all the time in the world."

They moved on, past the stairs and toward the elevator. Travis knew why they weren't taking the stairs; the steps were visible from the front entrance. The elevator, on the other hand, was well hidden.

"Where's the security guard?" Andy whispered. Travis hadn't realized that his head had popped up and he was watching. Travis's hand was still on Nish's head, holding him down. But now Nish was pushing up again.

"I don't know," said Travis.

"Maybe already up there," Nish said. "Maybe he went ahead to disconnect another alarm system."

"We'll wait one minute," Travis said, "then go."

It was a long minute. Travis could feel the tension. Usually, when he felt like this, he'd be chewing a fingernail. But now he didn't even feel the urge.

"Let's go!"

Andy pushed up on the tailgate and it swung silently out and up. The three of them scrambled out. Nish set the gate back down, careful not to let it close all the way.

They began moving very quietly down the hallway when Travis thought he heard a thumping. *Was it his heart coming right through his chest?* He signalled for them all to stop, and listened. There it was again.

"Let's check this out first," he said, turning.

The three Screech Owls headed back down the hall, and the thumping grew louder. Further on, they could see a door almost closed. The thumping continued, then stopped.

"Let's get outta here!" said Nish.

Travis forced himself to tip-toe closer.

He crept up to the door and peered into the small room. *There were two security guards inside, both tied up and gagged!* One of them must have been pounding his feet on the floor.

Travis's first instinct was to untie them, but then he realized that one of them had to be the guard who'd let the robbers in.

Had they double-crossed him? Or what if he'd been tied up as part of the plan? So no one would suspect him? Maybe he was still with the robbers?

And which one was he?

Travis raced back to Andy and Nish.

"What is it?" Nish hissed.

"They tied up two guards," Travis told him.

"Shouldn't we untie them?" asked Andy.

"Maybe one of them's working with the robbers – we can't take the chance."

Andy and Nish thought about it for a second and then realized the dilemma.

"We're going to have to pull this off ourselves," Travis said.

## 17

TRAVIS'S FIRST INCLINATION WAS TO HEAD FOR THE elevator, the same way he and Nish had gone when they first bumped into the robbers. But elevators make noise. Besides, it was already up a floor, having taken the two thieves up.

"We've got to use the stairs," Travis whispered.

Neither questioned him. In the dim security lights, he could see both Nish and Andy nod.

"Keep your heads down and go fast, and not a sound," Travis said.

Travis went first, low and scrambling up along the side of the stairs. From the top he could see the Great Hall where the trophies were. The elevator was to his right, down the short corridor where they had first encountered the robbers.

Nish came up, then Andy, each crouching low. He could hear them breathing. Travis had them all wait a moment until they calmed down.

They could hear noise from the vault area. The big doors were still open, and the robbers were talking.

"You think somebody's really going to pay a

million bucks ransom for a piece of old tin like this?" It was the darker one with the scar.

"This hockey-mad country?" the ponytail said. "You could get whatever you asked."

"Can't you hurry it up?"

"Just relax, okay. We move too fast, we trigger the secondary alarms. It's gonna take twenty minutes to do this right."

A power tool started up. A saw? A drill? It was difficult to say. Travis turned and looked at Andy and Nish. They looked back at him, waiting for instructions.

Travis felt a strange sensation. He thought he might actually know what to do.

"Follow me," he whispered, and ducked back down the stairs.

At the bottom they caught their breath again. Nish and Andy waited for Travis to talk.

"We're going to block the elevator," said Travis.

"How? It's already up there," said Nish.

"We'll block it with a hockey stick," Travis said. "Get a good straight one out of a display case. You can handle that part, Nish. Bring the stick over and call down the elevator – I don't think they'll hear it with all the noise they're making – and then jam the door open."

"What good will that do?"

"If the door can't close, they won't be able to call it up again and they'll have to use the stairs."

Both Nish and Andy thought about it a moment, then nodded.

"Get going," Travis said, and Nish ducked away, still staying low to the ground.

"C'mon with me," Travis said to Andy.

He scooted in the same direction Nish had gone, with Andy right behind him. When they came to the minivan, Travis stopped.

"Very quietly open the doors – we're taking Mom and Dad."

Andy glanced at him, not understanding, but said nothing. Travis seemed to know what he was doing and Travis was in charge.

The dummies were strapped in, but pulled out fairly easily, and Travis, with Mom over his shoulder, turned and scurried back toward the stairs. Andy, carrying Dad, hurried along behind.

At the bottom of the stairs, Travis stopped and listened. He could still hear the whir of power tools. He looked over toward the elevator and saw Nish, with a hockey stick in one hand, pushing the button to call the elevator.

"Bring Dad over here," Travis said.

Andy dumped him beside Mom.

"Can you bring both kids now?" Travis asked.

He nodded and hurried away, back to the van.

Travis sat down, breathing hard.

What now?

## 18

BEFORE ANDY CAME BACK WITH THE TWO SMALLER dummies, Travis was well into his plan. He'd taken one of the rolls of shin-pad tape out of Nish's bag and was putting it across the stairs about three-quarters of the way down and low to the ground. The cloudy tape did not show up in the dim light from the distant entrance way.

"It's done," whispered Nish, who came back just as Andy emerged from the darkness with the two kid dummies and plunked them down beside their parents.

Nish gave Travis a puzzled look.

"You'll see," said Travis. "You think you could get jackets and caps from the security guards? Maybe flashlights?"

Nish swallowed hard. "Alone?"

Travis looked at him, waiting.

Nish swallowed again. "I'll try."

He hurried off, past the minivan, past the Richard exhibit where he'd found the perfectly straight Love & Bennett stick, and on to the partially closed door to the room where they had found the guards.

He stopped to gather his courage. He breathed in twice, deeply, then gritted his teeth, stepped up to the door, and pulled it open.

The two security guards were sitting on the floor. Their feet and hands were tied and tape was plastered over their mouths. All he could see was their eyes: wondering, frightened, puzzled, anxious.

He couldn't help himself. "Sorry, boys – looking for the Tie Domi exhibit."

The two security guards looked at him as if he'd just dropped in from outer space. They had just started their evening snack when the robbers had come in. Luckily for Nish, both had removed their uniform jackets and placed them over the backs of folding chairs. One hat was hanging up, the other on the floor. He grabbed the hats and jackets and looked around for flashlights.

There was a small cupboard at the back of the room. He opened it. Inside were several big, silver flashlights and a bullhorn, just like the ones used on television for armed stand-offs. Perfect.

It was hard to carry everything. He had to put one cap on his head, then he looped the jackets over one shoulder and gathered up two flashlights and the bullhorn. The only way he could carry the second cap was to put the hard plastic peak in his mouth and bite down.

He pulled the cap out of his mouth for a moment. "I'll try not to slobber," he told the guards, who were still looking at him as if he were crazy. He bit down again, and with his arms and hands and mouth full, waddled quickly back to where Travis and Andy were finishing up the tape job on the stairs. When the other boys saw what Nish was bringing, they grinned. "Perfect," said Andy.

Travis looked around. The angle was just right; anything seen from the stairs would have the dim light in the corridor behind it and only show up as a silhouette.

"Get the jackets and caps on Mom and Dad," Travis said.

The two other boys struggled to put the jackets on, then the caps. Nish had to pound one cap down onto Dad. "Fathead," he whispered.

They moved Mom and Dad, now "Police" Officers Mom and Dad, out into the light of the corridor. Then Travis took the two kid dummies – whom they had named Data and Sister – and placed them behind a low exhibit on the opposite side. Again, with dim light behind them and nothing but a sweeping flashlight in front, they might appear to be crouching officers, waiting. Travis hoped so.

"Nish," Travis said, "you and I'll have to work the dummies. Andy – we want your deepest voice for the loudspeaker."

Andy looked shocked. "What'll I say?"

"You'll know. Just make it convincing."

## 19

THE WHINING OF THE POWER TOOL CAME TO AN abrupt stop. The silence was overwhelming – more frightening than anything Travis had experienced this scary evening.

The boys waited for several minutes, breathless, but there was nothing. No sound. No movement.

Travis could not understand what was happening. Were the robbers already gone? Was there another way out? He hadn't considered that possibility. The boys' whole plan depended on the crooks having to come back down the stairs when they discovered the elevator wasn't working.

"*Pssst!*" Travis called to Nish, and signalled for him to follow.

The two Screech Owls stepped carefully over the tape and ran quickly to the top of the stairs, where they crouched, waiting.

Travis thought he could hear something! A rustle. A grunt. The boys edged silently closer until they could peek into the vault.

Nish let out a slight gasp.

The robbers had only just got the Stanley Cup

off its stand. The ponytail was holding a sack open and the smaller robber was lowering it in. They'd be leaving any moment!

Travis and Nish hurried back down the stairs, careful to step over the shin-pad tape once more. Travis gave Andy the thumbs-up to let him know everything was okay and to get ready. Nish scooted back to his post.

The robbers were moving along the upper hall now. The boys went silent. Nish held onto the dad dummy for dear life for fear the figure would fall and the flashlight clatter across the floor. Travis was afraid to breathe.

They could hear the robbers, angry.

"What the hell's going on?"

They had obviously pushed the elevator button and nothing had happened. Travis could hear the propped-open elevator door bouncing lightly back and forth as it tried to close, but the stick was holding it. The elevator was going nowhere.

"C'mon, we'll use the stairs."

*Good*, Travis thought, *exactly what we want*.

Travis's heart could have accompanied a rock band. It was pounding so hard he thought it might be echoing off the walls. He thought maybe he could hear Nish's heart as well. And Andy's.

In fact Nish was so afraid of making a sound his heart wasn't even beating. He was hugging the dad dummy and holding onto the flashlight, and he had shut his eyes so tight he swore he could hear his eyelids squeak. He imagined the robbers suddenly coming to a halt, one of them holding up his hand and saying to the other: *"Did you hear that? Sounded like a kid's eyelid, didn't it?"*

Andy was crouched down behind an exhibit, his thumb about to flick the switch on the bull-horn. He was praying the robbers would knock themselves out on the stairs after they hit the tape – anything so long as he didn't have to go through with Travis's plan. He imagined flicking the switch and standing up and nothing whatsoever coming out of his mouth. Either nothing at all or some high-pitched squeak as if he were still in kindergarten: *"Put your hands up, Mr. Bad Guy, or I'll tell the teacher on you!"*

But there was no more time for wild imaginings. The robbers were on the stairs. The big one, the one with the ponytail, had the bulging sack over his back. The little one with the scar had a black bag – the power tools.

They came down quicker than Travis expected. A quarter of the way. Half way. Three quarters of the way, and they hit the tape together.

*"Aaaaarrrrghhhhhhhhh!!!"* the ponytail shouted.

*"Geeeez!!"* screamed the scar-face.

## 20

THE SOUND WAS LIKE AN EXPLOSION. TRAVIS FORGOT all about his heart. He jumped up as the two robbers hit the tape. They fell face-first, the power tools clattering, the Stanley Cup ringing as it hit the hard floor of the lower hall.

The robbers rolled a couple of times before settling in a heap at the bottom. Both seemed out cold – for a moment. Then they started swearing – worse than Travis had ever heard on a hockey rink – and began moving.

"FACE DOWN ON THE FLOOR!" a huge voice boomed. "NNNNOOOOWWW!!"

Travis spun around, thinking for a moment that the police actually had come. But it was Andy – his voice as deep and powerful and commanding as Travis had ever heard in his life. He almost hit the floor face-first himself.

A big beam of impossibly bright light swept over the two bewildered, swearing robbers. It blinded them, then bounced about the room, sweeping quickly over the two kid dummies so it appeared, just for a fraction of a second, that there were more "cops" present than just the two standing in the entrance hall.

Nish was very effective with his flashlight. He used it to make it seem that there was movement and to show that there were people there, but never let it linger. Every time he bounced it away from the robbers he turned it quickly back on them again, straight into their eyes, so all they could see was what must have looked like one big car headlight coming at them. Travis started to do the same with his light.

"I SAID ON YOUR FACE. MOVE IT!!"

Both robbers did exactly as they were told. They rolled, groaning and swearing, over onto their stomachs, faces down toward the floor but still straining to look up.

All they saw was the blinding flashlights.

"BEND YOUR FEET UP!! HANDS BEHIND THE BACK!! RIGHT NOW, MISTER! MOVE!"

This was Travis's signal. His heart skipped as he moved out from the shadow of the stairs and approached the robbers from behind.

"FACES DOWN!!" Andy shouted in his deepest voice. His voice was filling the room. It frightened even Travis, who knew where it was coming from.

"DIG YOUR NOSES INTO THE FLOOR, AND NOWWW!!"

The robbers, still cursing, did as they were told. Travis, careful to stay directly behind them so they couldn't see, quickly taped their hands and feet together with a roll of shin-pad tape. He went through two rolls before the ponytailed one turned and caught a glimpse of him.

"What the hell?! It's a kid!!"

The scar-face also twisted to see, his eyes bulging. "Ehhh?! What the . . . ?"

When they realized the person doing the tying-up was Travis Lindsay, captain of the Screech Owls, not Chief of the Metropolitan Toronto Police Force, they began twisting like fish at the bottom of a boat. Neither could move his hands or feet, but they could still scream.

"You little . . ."

"You take this tape off right now, you little jerk – or else!!"

Nish came running up now, suddenly brave. He had the security officer's cap on and was waving the flashlight. He had Dad over his shoulder. He tossed him toward the robbers.

"Stay with them, Officer Dummy!" Nish ordered.

When the two robbers saw they had been fooled by a dummy, they began twisting and cursing even more.

Andy came running out from his hiding place holding the loudspeaker.

"NO SWEARING!" Andy ordered. That only made them curse all the more.

"Such mouths!" Nish said, shaking his head in a disapproving manner.

"Trav," he called. "You got any of that tape left?"

Travis nodded, pulled half-a-roll out of his pocket, and tossed it to Nish. Nish put down the flashlight and went over to the ponytail. Standing behind him, he pulled out a length of the tape and tried to fit it over the robber's screaming mouth.

"Now, now, now," Nish said in his best teacher's voice. "This is for your own good."

It took him several tries, but finally he hit the robber's mouth and the screaming and swearing was partly muffled. He continued to loop the tape around the robber's head, careful not to cover his nose, and soon he was silent, but still furiously squirming.

Nish moved over and did the same to the scar-face. Soon there was only the sound of the tape coming off the roll. The sound, Travis thought, of a hockey dressing room. How appropriate!

The two robbers were trussed and ready for pick-up. All they needed was the police to come – but Nish wasn't through. He was scrambling after the sack. He picked up his big flashlight and threw it to Travis.

"Work the spotlight!" he shouted.

Travis hadn't a clue what Nish meant.

Nish reached into the sack and pulled out the Stanley Cup. He checked it. A new dent, perhaps, but nothing more. He lifted it up and kissed it, just like the victorious NHL players do.

He then hoisted the Stanley Cup high over his head and began pretending he was skating about the hall with it. "My spotlight!" he yelled out. Travis turned on the flashlight and shone it on Nish. It *was* just like a spotlight!

Nish completed a circuit of the hall, blowing kisses into the stands, blowing kisses at the two squirming robbers, bowing, kissing the Stanley Cup.

He then took the cup and, very carefully, set it on the step behind the taped-up robbers. He kissed it one more time.

"Let's get outta here!" Nish said.

Travis had two more things to do. With Nish's flashlight, they went back down the hall to where the two security officers were still tied up and taped silent. They stared and made muffled sounds as the boys came in, but the three had no intention of loosening them, even if one was totally innocent.

Travis rooted around the room until he found a piece of cardboard and a black felt pen. Then he made a quick sign:

## ONE OF THESE GUARDS WAS
## WORKING FOR THE ROBBERS.

He turned and showed it to the guards. One looked fiercely at him, the other looked surprised at the other guard. Travis was pretty sure he knew which one was guilty, but he still couldn't take a chance. He propped up the sign on a chair and they left the room.

At the exit the guard had opened for the two robbers, Travis found a fire alarm and set it off. The security alarms were probably all disengaged, but the fire alarm still worked. It began to ring throughout the Hockey Hall of Fame and it would be ringing at the nearest fire hall. In a few moments fire trucks would begin arriving.

"Let's go," he said.

# 21

FROM THE SOUND OF THE CHEERING, TRAVIS COULD tell that the Toronto Towers were already on the ice. They were the home team, and their parents and fans had filled up the lower seats of Maple Leaf Gardens. This was to be the highlight of the Little Stanley Cup, and even a camera crew from TSN was here. Player introductions and floods between periods. The real thing.

And yet it couldn't compare to what Travis already felt inside. Travis and Nish and Andy had made it back before curfew. They had told Willie, who didn't believe them until Nish found the news channel and there was a brief report on a foiled break-in at the Hockey Hall of Fame. They made him swear he wouldn't tell anyone.

In the morning the attempted robbery was front-page news – complete with a composite sketch of the three youngsters who had apparently been involved somehow but had slipped away into the night. The descriptions had been given by one of the tied-up security guards – Travis presumed the innocent one – but the sketch of Travis looked nothing like him whatsoever. Nor did the drawing of Andy. Nish, on the other hand, was . . . well, Nish was Nish.

Muck had been reading the paper when they came down. He had the story laid out on his lap and he kept looking at the drawings and looking up at Nish. But Nish never let on. "Sleep good, Coach?" he asked as he passed by.

If Muck suspected anything, he wasn't letting on. He didn't speak to them until just before the game, when he pulled a piece of paper out of his jacket pocket and announced, "I have a letter to read to you."

Dear Screech Owls,

Please accept our sincere apologies for what we did to you all. We are very sorry about what happened.

What we did was wrong and we know it. We don't really know why we did it, just that it happened and we were very, very lucky to be given another chance by the manager of the Hockey Hall of Fame.

We hurt a lot of people by our actions. We hurt ourselves by betraying those who trusted us: our parents, our coaches, and our team-mates. We hurt the Screech Owls by causing the team to be short players when you were all counting on us. We cost you all a chance to see the Leafs play.

We know we can't bring back the game, but we are all going to try to earn this trust back. We hope one day you will have us all back on the team, because that is where we want to be, more than anywhere else in the world. We love being Screech Owls and we're proud to be Screech Owls.

Thank you for listening to us.

Yours sincerely,

Larry Ulmar (Data)
Fahd Noorizadeh
Wilson Kelly

P.S. Beat those Towers!

Muck folded the letter, put it in his pocket, and walked out of the room without another word.

Travis pulled his sweater over his head, making the worst possible face at Nish as he was momentarily hidden from view. He pulled on his helmet and picked up his gloves.

"Let's go!" the captain of the Screech Owls shouted as he stood up.

## 22

TRAVIS FIGURED IT WAS AN IMPOSSIBLE TASK. THE
Toronto Towers were ahead 3–1 by the end of
the first period. The Screech Owls simply didn't
have the depth on the bench. Nish was playing,
and giving everything he had, but he was slowed
down by his bad ankle and had been on for two
of the Toronto goals.

Muck didn't seem alarmed. At the break he
simply went over the forechecking plan on his
little blackboard. "It's coming," Muck said. "It's
coming."

In the second period a pass hit Travis on the
shin pad. The puck bounced ahead and over the
defenceman's sweeping stick, but the defender
was quick enough to wrap an arm around Travis,
blocking him from the puck.

No matter – Dmitri had it. He flew down the
ice, faked a pass to Derek coming in from the left,
and fired a shot along the ice that went in under
the goaltender's stick. 3–2, Toronto Towers.

It remained 3–2 into the third. Travis looked
toward Nish at the far end of the bench. He was
bent over, holding his ankle, and there were tears

falling off his cheek. He was in terrible pain but had said nothing. And Muck, standing behind him, hadn't noticed. When Muck touched the back of Nish's sweater, he jumped right over the boards. He was going to give everything he had.

Nish tried a rush and made it to centre. A Tower hit him and the puck lay, untouched, at centre ice, where Liz picked it up and made a magnificent (was it accidental?) spinnerama move that took her around a check and created a two-on-one with Andy Higgins.

Liz hit Andy inside the blueline and Andy tried the big slap shot that usually caused Muck to roll his eyes. But for once the stick connected perfectly. The puck blew right through the Towers' goaltender's glove. 3–3 – *tied*.

## 23

MUCK HAD ONE TIME-OUT AND HE CALLED IT THE moment the Screech Owls tied the score. The players all gathered around him, waiting. Muck just stared at them.

"Just keep it up," Muck said.

That was all, *Just keep it up*. Why would he call a time-out? Travis wondered. Just to make the Towers think he had a master plan? Just to put them off? Travis had long ago given up trying to figure out Muck.

The referee's whistle blew. Travis's line was to take the face-off. Nish was on, wincing as he stood waiting for the puck to drop. Travis looked back at him and had never been so proud of his crazy friend.

Derek won the face-off and blocked off the Toronto centre. Travis was able to get his stick on the puck and slide it back to Nish, who fired low and hard, but not at the net. Instead, the puck flew at Dmitri, who simply turned his stick blade down and let the puck hit it and glance straight into the open net.

4–3, Screech Owls!

The Owls pounced on Dmitri, and also Nish, who had made the play.

*"Watch it!"* Nish kept shouting, to no avail. He didn't want anyone dumping him on his bad ankle. He shouldn't have been scurrying around the night before at the Hockey Hall of Fame, Travis thought. He should have been in bed, resting, just as Muck wanted.

The Owls held the lead until the final minute, when the Toronto Towers pulled their goaltender for a face-off in the Owls' end.

"Don't Panic!" Muck hollered from the bench. He had his hands over his mouth to make a megaphone. He sounded like Andy on the portable loudspeaker.

But they did. Derek lost the face-off, the puck went out to the point, Travis tried to block the shot and the defender simply stepped around him as Travis slid out past the blueline. It was now six-on-four for the Towers. The defenceman shot, the puck fell in a scramble of players, and a Toronto player put it in on the backhand.

4–4, tie game.

Dmitri had one more chance before the horn went, but lost the puck on the deke. The Towers were halfway back down the ice when time ran out.

Overtime.

## 24

"I CAN'T!" NISH SAID, HIS VOICE CRACKING.

Muck was leaning over his best defenceman. He had just asked Nish if he could take another shift. Muck had now seen the pain Nish was in, and he wouldn't make him. He patted his back while Nish buried his head below the boards.

Derek and Travis and Dmitri started the overtime, with Willie and Lars on defence. They didn't have Nish anymore. They didn't have Data. They didn't have Wilson. They didn't have Fahd.

The puck had barely dropped when it was over. Derek poked the puck ahead, but the Towers' best defenceman picked it up, stepped around Derek and pounded the puck off the boards so it floated in behind Willie, who turned too slowly to catch the swift winger breaking in. It was a design play, a plan, and the Towers had pulled it off perfectly.

The winger came flying in on Jennie, who in desperation lunged toward him, swinging her stick to poke-check him as she went down. But he had too much reach and too good an angle, and in a flash he was in behind her, dropping the puck in the net as if it were the easiest task in the world.

Maple Leaf Gardens went crazy! The Towers' bench emptied and the team piled on their scorer and their goaltender. Coaches, managers, parents leapt over the boards – the scene was as crazy as when a team wins the Stanley Cup.

The Screech Owls were crushed. They came and comforted Jennie, who could only shrug. No one blamed her, of course. It was a *team* loss. Muck wrapped a big arm around her neck and hugged her, face-mask and all. With her mask still on, no one could tell if she was crying.

But you could tell with Nish. He was limping on the ice, his ankle stiff and useless. Tears were rolling down his face and dropping onto his sweater. He couldn't help it. He didn't even bother wiping the tears away.

The Little Stanley Cup was on the ice, and Doug Gilmour – the Leafs' captain! – was coming on to present it. Travis looked at Doug Gilmour, who caught his eye and gave him a wink and a thumbs-up sign. *He had recognized him.*

They handed the Little Stanley Cup to Doug Gilmour, and he presented it to the Toronto Towers' captain, who lifted it over his head to the roar of the crowd. Triumphant, he began skating with it around the rink.

Travis felt a little tap on his shoulder. He turned. It was Nish, still crying, but now smiling through the tears as they both watched the Towers' captain hoisting the Little Stanley Cup.

"I prefer the original, myself," said Nish.

Travis couldn't help himself. He began to laugh. Andy Higgins, standing close by, began laughing as well.

**THE END**

THE NEXT BOOK IN THE SCREECH OWLS SERIES

*The Screech Owls' Northern Adventure*

by Roy MacGregor

The Screech Owls are on the road again, headed for a northern adventure that will test more than their skill at hockey!

Jesse Highboy's dad has invited the Screech Owls to James Bay to play as guests in the First Nations Tournament, with teams of Native kids from all over the country taking part. The pressure is on the Screech Owls to live up to the honour and play some good hockey, but they're also looking forward to learning a bit about the traditional ways of the North.

Jesse leads the team on a trip to the Highboy Hunt Camp, run by his grandfather, who teaches them a thing or two about surviving in the northern wilderness. But when Travis, Nish, and Jesse get lost in the bush, they realize they're going to have to put their new-found knowledge to the test.

# Chapter 1

"I'M GONNA HURL!"

Five rows away, Travis Lindsay could hear Nish moaning into a pillow. He could hear him over the tinny pound of the Walkman hanging loosely off Data's bent ears as he dozed in the next seat. He could hear him over the clatter of the serving cart and the shouting coming from Derek and Dmitri as they played a game of hearts in the row behind. He could even hear Nish over the unbelievable roar of the engines.

How could anyone sleep at a time like this? Travis wondered, glancing at Data. This was the first time Travis had flown, and it hadn't been at all what he had imagined. This was no ten-minute helicopter lift at the fall fair; nor was it like the big, smooth passenger jet his father took once a month to business meetings in Montreal. This was three solid hours of howling engines, air pockets, and broken cloud. They were headed, it seemed, for the North Pole. They had all driven to Val d'Or, Quebec, the day before, and from there it was 1,500 kilometres further north by air to their final destination: Waskaganish, a native village on the shore of James Bay.

They were on a Dash 8, an aircraft that Data – who knew everything about computers and National Hockey League statistics, but nothing whatsoever about life – claimed could take off and land in the palm of your hand. This was an exaggeration, of course, but Travis had felt it wasn't far off when the cramped fifty-seat plane taxied out onto the runway, revved the engines hard once, and seemed to shoot straight off the ground into the low clouds.

Travis had barely taken a second breath by the time the plane rose through the clouds and into the sunshine hidden beyond. It was as if the cabin of the plane were being painted with melted gold. Blinded by the sudden light, Data lowered the window-shade, but Travis had reached across and raised it again. He wanted to see everything.

The pilot had come on the intercom and warned them that the flight might be bumpy and that he'd be leaving the seatbelt sign on. The flight attendant would have to wait before bringing out the breakfast cart.

The coaches and several parents, Travis's included, were sitting toward the back of the plane. Data's and Wilson's and Fahd's parents were all there. Perhaps they wanted to make sure nothing went wrong this time the way it had in Toronto.

The three boys hadn't missed a game or

practice since Muck let them come back at the end of a month-long suspension over the unfortunate shoplifting incident at the Hockey Hall of Fame. They'd apologized to the team and they'd missed a key tournament, and eventually Muck figured they'd learned their lesson. Travis knew they had. He'd talked to Data on the telephone almost every night during his suspension, and he knew that several times Data had been in tears.

Jesse Highboy was sitting directly across from Travis. Beside him were his father and mother and his Aunt Theresa, the Chief of Waskaganish. No one called her Theresa or even Mrs. Ottereyes – they all called her "Chief." She had come down to Val d'Or to welcome the Screech Owls, and now she was bringing them all to Northern Quebec for the First Nations Pee Wee Hockey Tournament, which would feature, for the first time, a non-native peewee hockey team: the Screech Owls.

Jesse's father had set it up. He had met with the team and parents and talked to them about the chance of a lifetime. The hockey would be a part of the trip, he had stressed, but the real reward would come in getting to experience the North and the native culture. All they had to do was get there. The people of Waskaganish were so pleased with the idea that they'd offered to put everyone up, players and parents, free of charge. No wonder so many hands had gone up when Mr. Highboy asked for a show of interest.

The Owls had held bottle drives and organized car washes, and the parents had worked so many bingos that Mr. Lindsay celebrated the end of them by burying his smoke-filled "bingo clothes" in a deep hole behind the garage. The team had read up on the North and were excited about what they had learned: the northern lights, caribou, traplines, the midnight sun.

"It's *spring*, not summer!" Willie Granger, the team trivia expert, had pointed out to those Owls, like Nish, who figured they'd never have to go to bed and could stay up all night long. "Day and night are just about equal this time of year – same as where we live." But no one expected anything else to be the same. No one.

Perhaps, Travis wondered, this was why Nish had been acting so oddly. In the weeks leading up to the trip, Nish had kidded Jesse mercilessly.

"Should I bring a bow and arrow?" Nish had asked. "Will we be living in teepees?"

Some of it had been pretty funny, Travis had to admit, but it left him feeling a bit uneasy. Travis knew that the general rule of a hockey dressing room was "anything goes," and certainly Jesse had handled Nish's cracks easily, laughing and shooting back insults, but Travis still found it intriguing that no one other than Nish took such shots.

No one expected teepees. But beyond that they didn't really know what to expect.

Chief Ottereyes and Air Creebec, the airline

that set up the charter, had put on a special break-fast for the Owls. Once the turbulence had settled enough, the flight attendant handed out a breakfast the likes of which no Screech Owl, Jesse Highboy excepted, had ever seen. There were tiny things like tea biscuits that Chief Ottereyes explained were "bannock – just like we cook up out on the trapline." And there was fish, but not cooked like anything Travis had ever seen at a fish-and-chip shop. This fish was dry and broke apart easily. At first Travis wasn't too sure, but when he tasted it he thought it was more like *candy* than fish. "Smoked whitefish," Chief Ottereyes said. "Smoked and cured with sugar."

"I got no knife and fork!" Nish had shouted from his seat.

Chief Ottereyes laughed: "You've got hands, haven't you?"

"Yeah."

"Clamp 'em over your mouth, then!" Wilson had called from the other side of the plane.

"This is traditional Cree food!" Chief Ottereyes had leaned forward and told Nish.

"I'll take a traditional Egg McMuffin, thank you!" Nish called back.

He wouldn't try the food. Instead, he'd dug down into the carry-on bag he had stuffed beneath his seat and hauled out three chocolate bars and sat stuffing his face with one hand while he used the other to hold his nose as though he couldn't stand the smell of the smoked fish.

They had just been finishing up this unusual breakfast when the plane rattled as if it had just hit a pothole. The "fasten your seatbelt" light flashed and the pilot had come on the intercom to tell the attendant to stop picking up the trays and hang on, they were about the enter some more choppy air.

"I'M GONNA HURL!"

With the plane starting to buck, the attendant was unable to move forward to help Nish in case he was, in fact, going to be sick. Instead, she passed ahead a couple of Gravol air-sickness pills, a juice to wash them down, and a barf bag in case the worst happened. Nish took the pills and soon began moaning.

After a while, when the plane began to settle again, Nish called out, "Can I get a blanket?"

Travis thought Nish was acting like a baby. The attendant handed over a blanket, and the players behind Nish tossed theirs over, too. He wrapped himself tight and pressed his face into the pillow, then closed his eyes and continued to moan.

The pilot took the plane to a higher altitude, and the flight once again smoothed out. Derek and Dmitri's card game started up again, the attendant completed her collection of the break-fast trays, and Nish moaned on.

Data stood up in the aisle. "I think he needs a

few more blankets!" he called out, grinning mischievously. "I can still hear him."

Blankets and pillows by the dozen headed in Data's direction. Even Muck, shaking his head in mock disgust, handed his over. Data, now helped by Wilson, stacked them on poor Nish until he could be neither seen nor heard.

"There," Data announced. "That ought to hold him."

Nish never budged. Travis figured he must have gone to sleep. He hoped he was able to breathe all right through the blankets, but it was nice not to have to listen to him any longer. Travis turned toward the window and thought about the tournament and how he would play. He felt great these days. Hockey was a funny game: sometimes when you didn't feel well but played anyway, you had the most wonderful game; sometimes when you felt fantastic, you played terribly.

He tried to imagine himself playing in Waskaganish, but he couldn't. He couldn't picture the rink. He couldn't imagine the village. He could not, for the first time in his life, even imagine the players on the other side. Would they be good players? Rough? Smart? Would they have different rules up here? No, they couldn't have. He was getting tired, too tired to think . . .

*". . . put your seats in the upright position, fasten your tables back, and ensure that all carry-on luggage is safely stowed under the seat in front of you. Thank you."*

The announcement and the sudden sense that something was happening woke Travis with a start. He could hear seats being moved, tables being fastened, excitement rising.

"I can see the village!" Derek shouted from behind.

Travis leaned toward the window. He could see James Bay stretching away like an ocean, the ice along the shore giving way to water that was steel grey and then silver where the sun bounced on the waves.

The plane was beginning to rock again. The plane came down low over the water, then began to bank back toward the village. Travis could see a hundred or more houses. He could see a church, and a large yellow building like a huge machine shed. The rink? He could see the landing strip on the right: one long stretch of ploughed ground.

Just then, they hit a huge air pocket. The plane banked sharply and seemed to slide through the air sideways before righting itself with a second tremendous jolt.

"HELP MEEEEEEEE!!"

Travis could hear Nish screaming over the roar of the engines and the landing gear grinding down into position. No one could go to him. They were landing.

"I'M DYINNNGGG!" Nish screamed from beneath his blankets.

The big plane came down and hammered into the ground, bounced twice, and settled, the engines roaring as the pilot immediately began to brake. The howl was extraordinary.

Nish moaned and cried until the plane slowed and turned abruptly off the landing strip toward an overgrown shed that had a sign, WASKAGANISH, over the doorway. There was a big crowd gathered. It seemed the whole town was out to greet the Screech Owls.

"HELP MEEEE!!" Nish moaned. Travis had never heard such a pathetic sound.

Finally, as the plane came to a halt, the attendant got up and began pulling off Nish's blankets, digging him out, until his big, red-eyed face was blinking up at her in surprise.

"I thought we'd crashed," he said, "and I was the only survivor." Everyone on the plane broke up.

The attendant just shook her head. Travis couldn't tell if she was amused or disgusted.

"You wouldn't want to survive," the Chief told him. "You'd never make it out of the bush alive, my friend."

Nish looked up, blinking. "I *wouldn't*?"

"Of course not," she said, then reached over and pinched Nish's big cheek.

"The Trickster eats fat little boys like you!"

Nish looked blank. What *was* she talking about?

## THE SCREECH OWLS SERIES